SAVING BREELY

BROTHERHOOD PROTECTORS YELLOWSTONE
BOOK FIVE

ELLE JAMES

TWISTED PAGE INC

SAVING BREELY

BROTHERHOOD PROTECTORS
YELLOWSTONE BOOK #5

New York Times & USA Today
Bestselling Author

ELLE JAMES

Dedicated to my dear friend Desiree Holt, the author who inspired me to keep going. She was an amazing woman, writer and friend. I was truly blessed to call her my friend.
Elle James

AUTHOR'S NOTE

Enjoy other military books by Elle James

Brotherhood Protectors Yellowstone
Saving Kyla (#1)
Saving Chelsea (#2)
Saving Amanda (#3)
Saving Liliana (#4)
Saving Breely (#5)
Saving Savvie (#6)
Saving Jenna (#7)

Visit ellejames.com for more titles and release dates
Join her newsletter at
https://ellejames.com/contact/

CHAPTER 1

"Moe, are you sure you don't need anyone to fly with you tonight?" Hank Patterson sat across the table at the Tumbleweed Tavern in Bozeman, Montana.

Morris "Moe" Cleveland shook his head. "I don't need a wingman. I have over a thousand hours. I've flown solo from Florida to Alaska and so many other places. A short hop to Denver is nothing."

"Yeah, but it's getting late," Hank insisted. "All I have to do is call Sadie, and I can go with you."

"Members of our team in West Yellowstone volunteered to come along for the ride, and I turned them down." Moe smiled. "I appreciate the offer. But, seriously, it's not necessary. I'm waiting for a call from the hospital."

"What you're doing is so important to the people on the receiving end," Hank said. "Losing a loved one is horribly painful, but the life that person's organs can sustain is a miracle. Life out of death." He shook his head. "We're lucky to have you as one of our Brotherhood Protectors."

Moe nodded. "Thank you for coming to our rescue in Afghanistan and giving us purpose in the civilian world."

"So, what's your plan?" Hank asked.

"As soon as they have the organs ready, I'll pick them up and head to the airport," Moe said. "The flight will take less than three hours. An ambulance will meet me at the airport to collect the ice chest. Then, I'll stay the night in Denver and head back tomorrow. Unless Stone has some work for me, I'm not in any hurry to return. So, you see, if I go by myself, I won't hold up anyone else from what they might need to do, and I won't have to hurry back tomorrow."

Hank grinned. "Okay. You've convinced me. I'm headed home. Sadie will be happy to have help getting Emma and McClain to bed." He motioned for the waitress. "If you need anything, let me know. Hopefully, you'll get to leave soon. There's a storm heading our way."

Moe nodded. "I have my eye on the forecast. It's not supposed to reach here or Denver until sometime after three in the morning. I should be in a hotel by then after delivering my cargo."

The red-haired waitress who'd introduced herself as Bea and had served them all evening approached. "Want another round?" she asked with a smile lighting up her pretty green eyes.

"Not for me," Hank said. "My friend might want another soda. I'd like to settle the bill so I can get on the road home to Eagle Rock."

She cocked an eyebrow in Moe's direction. "Want another? Or something stronger?"

Moe nodded. "Coffee. Black. No cream or sugar."

She chuckled, the throaty sound registering in Moe's gut. "I guess that's stronger," she said. "I was thinking more along the lines of alcohol."

Hank pushed to his feet and tossed several twenties on the table. He grabbed his cowboy hat and clapped a hand on Moe's back while shooting a grin toward Bea. "Our friend is flying. No alcohol for him."

Bea's eyebrows rose into the coppery swath of hair hanging over one side of her forehead. "Does it make you airsick?"

Moe shook his head. "No, but as the pilot, I can't drink and fly."

Her smile spilled across her face, making the room seem so much brighter. "Oh. That makes more sense." She gathered the twenties. "I'll be right back with the coffee and your change."

Hank held up a hand. "No change."

"Thank you, but that's too much." Bea held out one of the twenties. "Would you like a coffee to take with you?"

Hank curled his hand around hers and the twenty. "Please. You've been very attentive and kind. I insist." He released her hand. "No, thank you for the coffee. It keeps me awake when I should sleep. With a baby in the house, you sleep when you can."

Moe grinned. "Sounds like when we were on missions in the military. I can remember catching a catnap in the mountains of Afghanistan while waiting for dark and our cue to move out on an extraction."

Hank laughed. "Babies and children are like maneuvering through a minefield in enemy territory."

"When you put it like that, I'm surprised anyone would want to have kids." Moe shook his head.

"No kidding," Bea said. "Children are a huge responsibility, and so many variables are out of your control."

"Like their sleeping schedules," Hank said.

"Or when they get sick," Moe added.

"Or die," Bea murmured. "I'll be right back with your coffee." She turned away, the smile she'd shared with them gone. Her lips thinned, and the light her smile had generated was snuffed out.

A frown settled over Hank's face as he watched the waitress leave.

Moe pushed to his feet. "Thank you for taking the time to meet with me while I'm in Bozeman." He held out his hand.

Hank gripped it in a firm handshake. "I'm glad you let me know you'd be here. It's good to catch up with you. Since I had business in town anyway, it worked out." He released Moe's hand. "I need to get down to West Yellowstone more often. I'm glad to hear things are going well for our Yellowstone branch of Brotherhood Protectors."

"We're glad for the work and that you and your team came to our rescue when our government pulled out of Afghanistan." Moe shook his head.

"You'd have done the same for us," Hank said. "And you're doing us a favor. We have more work than we can handle. It's men like you, Stone, Carter and the others who have the skills needed to handle the missions that come our way."

Bea returned, carrying a mug and a carafe of steaming coffee.

Hank settled his cowboy hat on his head. "I'll leave you to your coffee. My wife will be happy I'm home tonight to help her with the little ones." Hank tipped his hat toward Bea and strode through the tavern toward the exit.

Moe sank into his seat, his gaze on the former Navy SEAL.

Bea's gaze followed Moe's for a moment and then

returned to him. "Are you and your friend in the military?"

Moe shook his head, his attention shifting to the waitress. "We were. Not anymore."

"Thank you for your service." Bea set the mug on the table and poured the rich, steaming liquid.

The scent filled the air. Moe inhaled deeply.

When Bea straightened, her smile was in place, if a little more reserved. "Is there anything else you'd like? My shift ends soon, and I don't want to leave you hanging."

Moe glanced around the tavern, noting the many empty tables. "Is it normally this slow?"

She shrugged. "On weeknights, the rush starts around five o'clock and ends near seven-thirty. People stop for a bite to eat and head home. Week-ends are crazy with customers here until we close at two in the morning."

"That makes for a long night," Moe said.

Her lips twisted in a wry smile. "I'm not complaining. The tips are good, and the people are usually friendly."

"Do you work here full-time?" Moe asked, purposely delaying her. He wanted to see her smile like she had the first time when she'd lit the room.

"I normally only work the weekends. I'm filling in for one of the girls who called in sick."

"Do you work somewhere else during the week?" he asked, curious about this petite red-haired woman with the moss-green eyes and a smattering of freckles across her nose.

Bea glanced away. "I have a day job during the week."

"Let me guess..." He tipped his head to the side and studied her. "You're a real estate agent, finding the perfect homes for your clients."

Bea lifted her chin. "If I was, would you hire me to find the home of your dreams?"

"Absolutely." He grinned. "If I lived in Bozeman."

Her brow puckered. "You're not from Bozeman?"

"No, I'm from San Antonio, Texas, where I joined the Air Force and let that fine establishment ship me all over the world. Sadly, I'm not from Beautiful Bozeman. I'm just here for the evening."

"Oh," she said. "That's too bad. I don't know many people here, and well...it would've been nice to make a new friend." She started to turn away with the carafe of coffee. "I'm not a real estate agent. Although I might give that a try if waiting tables doesn't work out."

"Wait." He touched her arm. "You have to give me at least two more chances to get it right."

Bea chuckled and turned back to him. "If you must. Go ahead."

"You're a private investigator, chasing after men cheating on their wives."

She snorted and pointed to her shoulder-length,

red hair swaying around her chin. "They'd spot me in a second with this mop of red hair."

Moe's eyes narrowed. "You're right. It is sexy and unique. I suppose a PI would have to blend into the background."

"Red hair is never sexy." She held up a finger. "Last chance."

"You're wrong. Your red hair is off-the-scale-sexy. Don't let anyone tell you it's not." He tapped a finger to his chin. "The pressure is on. I have to get it right this time or lose you forever."

"You can't lose what you don't have." She tipped her chin. "You don't have me."

"No." He grinned. "But I have your attention."

"Not for long."

"One more guess," he begged, "and I'll leave you alone."

Bea drew in a deep breath and let it out slowly. "Okay. One more."

He thought hard. What would a sassy, petite, gorgeous redhead do for a day job? The wattage of her genuine smile lit the room. When she'd spoken of a child dying, the shadows beneath her eyes and that haunted look had pulled at Moe's heart. She'd experienced loss. Of a child?

"You're kind, caring and help people in need." He slapped his hand on the table. "That's it. You're a saint or a nun."

Bea choked on a laugh. "You're so far off. But that

one was worth the chuckle."

"You're not a nun?" Moe wiped his hand across his forehead. "Whew. Thank goodness, because I was having very unsaintly thoughts about your sexy red hair."

She shook her head slowly. "Does this technique ever work for you?"

He raised his eyebrows. "Technique?"

Her lips pressed together. "This pickup line of 'guess your occupation?'"

"You tell me," he said with a wink.

"Sorry. You'd have been better off just asking me out."

"Alas, I'm only here for an undisclosed amount of time that could end at any minute."

"Sounds very clandestine." Bea shook her head. "I have some cleaning to do before I leave. It was nice talking to you. Too bad you're not in town for longer. I could have used a friend."

"So, you're not from Bozeman either?"

She shook her head. "I've only been here for a couple of weeks."

"Where are you from?"

Her lips tightened.

"Bea!" a deep, male voice called out from the swinging door to the kitchen.

"Coming," Bea responded. "Gotta go. Nice talking to you. Have a happy life." She spun and hurried toward the man wearing a white apron and holding a mop in one hand.

Bea paused on the way past the bar to set the pot of coffee on a heating element. Then she hurried toward the man in the apron, grabbed the mop handle and darted around the big guy into the kitchen.

A stab of guilt gnawed at Moe's gut. He'd kept her talking when she was supposed to be working. He hoped he hadn't gotten her into too much trouble.

He sipped the coffee, liking how it warmed his throat and insides. He'd need the caffeine for the flight to Denver. Thankfully, it wasn't a very long flight. He glanced at this watch. It was getting late. At any moment, he expected the call telling him to go to the hospital to collect his biological cargo.

He downed another swallow of the hot coffee, scorching his tongue and throat. Moe set the cup aside, his thoughts on Bea.

Without her stimulating presence, the tavern had lost its appeal. He might as well head to the hospital and be there when they were finally ready.

He pushed back from the table, rose and glanced toward the swinging kitchen door, willing Bea to emerge.

When she didn't, he sighed and headed for the exit. There was only one table left with two customers finishing their meals. The tavern would close soon.

Moe stepped outside, turned his face to the nearly

full moon, drew a deep breath of clear, cool air and let it out slowly.

He hadn't intended his discussion with Bea as a pickup line. Thinking back over what he'd said, he realized it had been pretty cheesy. Had he insulted her? He glanced at his watch.

If he hurried, he might catch her before she left and apologize for holding her up with a less-than-stellar attempt at conversation.

Moe turned around in time to see the last couple leaving the tavern and the man in the white apron following behind them to lock the door. He flipped the sign in the window from OPEN to CLOSED. He turned and started stacking chairs upside down on the tables.

Moe's heart sank. So much for going back inside to catch her and apologize. Then he realized Bea hadn't come out the front door. More likely, she'd leave through a rear entrance.

If he hurried, he might catch her. Moe turned to his right, strode toward the corner of the rustic tavern and slipped into an alley between the tavern and the art gallery to the east.

The sound of a motor vehicle engine revving made Moe move faster. He wasn't sure why he felt so compelled to see the waitress once more. He'd never been that attracted to redheads.

Bea was different. She was a diminutive, fiery figure with compassion and chutzpah. Yeah, he'd catch her, apologize and ask her out. He didn't live in Bozeman, but he had the plane and could fly back when he wanted.

It wouldn't happen if he didn't catch her before she left.

CHAPTER 2

"THAT DUDE BOTHERING YOU?" Stan Morgan, the cook and proud owner of the Tumbleweed Tavern, held the swinging door for Bea to enter the kitchen.

She grabbed the mop and ducked past Stan. "No, I think he was flirting with me."

"Think?" Stan snorted and crossed to the grill. He grabbed a scraper and pushed it across the metal surface once and paused. "Either he was, or he wasn't."

Breely Brantt, known only as Bea Smith at the tavern, fought the smile threatening to spread across her face. "He was."

Stan straightened to his full six feet four inches of barrel-chested toughness and glared. "I can go out there and mop the floor with him, if you like."

"I don't like," Breely said.

His huge stature might have frightened others,

but Breely knew the man's bark was much worse than his bite. Stan had a big heart for the people he liked. And he'd taken a liking to Breely the moment she'd started working at the Tumbleweed Tavern. He'd murmured something about his granny having red hair, and that had been enough for him.

Breely cringed at the thought of big ol' Stan stomping on the flirt. The man wasn't even a foot taller than Breely, who measured five feet tall in her bare feet. That would make him less than six feet tall and subject to a severe beating at the hands of Stan "The Man" Morgan, former competitive wrestler turned cook and tavern owner.

Breely carried the mop to the corner of the kitchen where the bucket of water stood. She shoved the mop into the bucket and lifted it into the press. Breely leaned on the handle to squeeze out the excess moisture. "No need to mop the floor with him. He was harmless and kind of cute." She ran the mop over the floor in front of the commercial refrigerators and then carried it back to the bucket.

Stan shook his head, his brow furrowing. "I don't like it. Customers gotta treat my staff with respect." He set the scraper on the grill and turned toward the dining room door. "I'm gonna have a talk with him."

Breely, dripping mop in hand, raced to catch Stan.

The big man beat her to the door, pushed it open and came to a complete stop.

Breely plowed into Stan, slipped on the water

dripping from the mop and almost crashed to the floor.

Stan's arm snapped out, and his hand clamped onto her arm and steadied her. "Chill," he ordered.

"How am I supposed to chill when my boss is about to go ballistic on a guy half his size?"

Stan chuckled. "He might be short to me, but he's still bigger than you."

Breely wedged herself between Stan and the door. "Everyone's bigger than me. You can't go out there and intimidate him. It's not nice."

Stan's stern countenance softened a little with his lips quirking on the corners. "Relax. Your guy just left." Her boss chuckled, returned to his grill and finished scraping it clean.

Breely let go of the breath she'd been holding, the tension in her body subsiding to be replaced by an unreasonable disappointment.

He'd said he would be leaving at any moment. Too bad he hadn't stuck around until she'd gotten off work. Breely hadn't been lying when she'd said she'd like to make a new friend.

Why she'd told him that, she wasn't sure. She'd met a number of people since she'd escaped to Bozeman to start her new life. Until her last customer of the evening, she hadn't met anyone she'd wanted to open up to about wanting a friend.

Was it because he'd said he wouldn't be there longer than the evening? Or was it because he wasn't that big or intimidating? Most guys stood head and shoulders above her, making her feel like a little girl. The flirt didn't make her feel like a little girl at all. In fact, he'd made her feel desirable, like the full-grown, mature woman she was.

He'd even called her red hair sexy.

She could forgive that lie because the tone of his voice and the smoldering look in his eyes had set her blood on fire, burning through her veins.

No, he wasn't the typical muscle-bound hulk of a man most women swooned over. His friend, though older, fit that description to the letter.

The flirt was short and wiry with black hair and brown eyes. When he'd touched her arm, his hand had been firm but gentle.

Breely could imagine those hands smoothing over more than her arm. Her core heated. She could imagine the flirt lying over her. He wouldn't crush her beneath him. Making love to him would be a partnership in pleasure.

Wow. How long had it been since she'd slept with a man?

Obviously too long if a chance encounter with a guy with a terrible pickup line turned her on. She shook her head and got back to the business at hand.

She quickly finished mopping the kitchen, emptied the bucket and rinsed it clean.

Stan had filled the dishwasher with a tray of plates and glasses and started the cycle. He wiped his hands on his apron, walked toward the swinging door and stopped before pushing through to the dining room. "If you want me to walk you to your car," he said, "you'll have to wait for me to lock the front door."

"That won't be necessary. I can walk by myself," Breely said. "I'll dump the trash on my way out."

Stan's brow furrowed. "You sure you can't wait?"

She smiled. "I'll be fine," she assured him. "Thanks anyway."

Stan glanced through the crack in the door. "Last customer is leaving. I'm going to lock the door. Night, Bea."

"Goodnight, Stan." Breely grabbed the heavy trash bag and lugged it toward the back door. She had to back into the door to keep it open as she pulled the big bag through it.

Once on the other side, she let the door swing closed, turned toward the huge trash bin and frowned.

A van stood between her and her goal. A quiver of uneasiness slithered across her skin, raising the fine hairs and gooseflesh on her arms.

Instinct made her spin and reach for the back door. The trash bag stood in the way.

Before she could move around it or shove the bag to the side, a door sliding open sounded behind her.

Her heartbeat kicked into hyperdrive. She grabbed the big bag and flung it around her body and behind her. As she turned, she counted two men, both wearing black clothing and ski masks, as they leaped from the van.

One man hooked his arm around her waist and dragged her backward.

When Breely drew a quick breath to scream, a large hand clamped over her mouth, muffling the sound.

She dug her heels into the pavement, then twisted and turned in an attempt to break free from the man's hold. Her feet were yanked out from under her by the other man. Together, they carried her toward the open door of the van.

Breely fought, twisting and bucking against the holds they had on her. She managed to pull one foot free and kicked hard, landing her heel in the masked face of the man struggling to hold onto her other foot.

He cursed and relaxed his hold.

Her feet hit the ground.

When the man holding her around her middle lifted her toward the open van door, Breely pulled her knees up and planted her feet on the doorframe.

Her captor cursed. "Get her damned feet," he hissed.

Breely had to choose between kicking out or continuing to brace her legs against the van doorframe.

The man she'd kicked in the face slammed his

arm down on her kneecaps, breaking her toehold on the outside of the van.

As soon as her feet fell, her captor shoved her into the van.

Breely screamed, planted her feet on the metal floor and launched herself at the two men blocking her escape.

The one who'd carried her to the van backhanded her across the cheek, sending her flying backward into the van. She lay stunned, gray fog closing around her.

The door slid closed, blocking what little light had filtered through the fog, plunging Breely into darkness.

A shout barely penetrated her consciousness. Something slammed against the metal door, rocking the metal floor beneath Breely. Again, something big slammed into the van, this time jerking Breely out of the fog.

Her head still fuzzy and her cheek aching, she pushed herself up onto her hands and knees and searched for another door on the other side of the van. There wasn't one. She crawled toward the sliding door.

Someone cursed. Again, something heavy rammed into the closed sliding door.

Breely reeled back and felt her way toward the van's rear, praying for doors at the back. With her hand on the side of the van, she crawled to the end, found door latches and tried to push them down. They didn't move.

More grunting and loud cracking sounds erupted outside the van.

Breely turned around, pushed to her feet and walked in a hunched position toward the front of the vehicle, stumbling once over debris in her way. When her fingers touched the back of the driver's seat, she almost cried in relief.

She had just eased one leg through the gap between the driver and passenger seats when the sliding door crashed open. "No," she cried and tried to slide the rest of the way into the seat.

Hands gripped her around the waist and dragged her out of the van.

"No!" she cried louder. "Help me! Please! Help!" Breely bucked and twisted, clawing at the hands now wrapped around her waist. "Let go of me."

"Shhh, Bea," a familiar voice cut through her panic. "It's okay. They're gone." The arms around her middle loosened.

Breely spun in the circle of the flirt's arms. "Oh, thank God." She flung her arms around his neck and buried her face against his chest.

He held her, gently stroking her back.

A door slammed open and a voice shouted, "Release her, you son of a bitch!" Stan yelled.

Breely's head snapped up in time to see Stan storming toward them, holding a rolling pin high above his head, aiming for the man holding her in his arms.

"No, Stan." Breely broke away from the man and planted herself between Stan and her rescuer. "It's okay."

"He attacked you." Stan still held the rolling pin over his head, his glare going over her shoulder to the man behind her.

Breely held up her hand. "No. He rescued me from the two men who attacked me." She looked around. "Where did they go?"

"When they saw that they weren't going to get into the van with you, they took off," the flirt said.

Stan's eyes narrowed. "You held off two men?"

The flirt shrugged. "They didn't know much about fighting. I knocked both of them out temporarily. When I went to the van to find Bea, one of them recovered enough to throw the other over his shoulder and take off. I had other priorities." He slipped an arm around Breely's waist. "Did they hurt you?" He turned her to face him and frowned. "What the hell?"

She gave a small laugh and touched her cheek. "One of them backhanded me. It doesn't hurt." She touched the bruised area and winced. "Much."

Anger burned in the flirt's dark eyes, making the brown closer to black. "The bastards. I should have finished them off."

Stan pulled his cell phone from his apron pocket,

punched three numbers and pressed the phone to his ear. "I'd like to report an attack on one of my employees. The attackers got away." He looked over at Breely. "What were they wearing?"

Breely pinched the bridge of her nose. "Black ski masks. I'm not exactly sure what else. Seems they were all in black."

"All in black and black ski masks," Stan relayed.

A siren wailed in the distance, moving closer.

"I hear the sirens now," Stan said. "No blood or broken bones that I can see. Yes, thank you." He ended the call and slipped his cell phone into his apron pocket. "The first responders and the sheriff are on their way."

Out of the van, and with the attackers gone, reaction set in. Breely trembled. The trembling became full body shaking, and her teeth rattled. The cool night air wasn't helping.

The flirt slipped an arm around her and pulled her against him. "Cold?" he asked.

She nodded, her teeth chattering. Clear Montana nights could be so very cold, even in the middle of summer. Her shaking was more than the chill in the air. She'd almost been kidnapped.

If not for this man holding her in the curve of his arm, she could be well on her way to wherever the two men had planned to take her.

Her rescuer rubbed his hands up and down her arm. "Is that better?" he asked, his tone low, soothing and making her shake for more reasons than the chill in the air and the shock of being jumped.

"Do you want me to stop?" he whispered, his breath warm against her ear.

She shook her head, turned her face into his chest and wrapped her arms around his waist.

His arms wrapped around her and held her securely against his hard frame. They stood together until the sheriff and an ambulance arrived.

The first responders hurried to Breely and extricated her from her rescuer's arms.

A surge of panic swept through her, and she brushed aside the first responder's hands to melt against the man who'd rescued her.

He held her while the medical technician took her vitals and suggested she take a short ride to the hospital for observation. "She could have a concussion," he suggested.

"I didn't black out all the way," Breely protested. "I'm fine. I just want to go home."

"I'll get you there," Moe promised. "But a trip to the hospital is a better option."

Breely looked to the sheriff. "Are we done here?" Her teeth were still clattering as she walked toward the position where she'd parked her Porsche sports car. When she reached for the door handle, her rescuer pulled her back. "Wait." He bent to inspect the tires. "They've been slashed."

"Why?" Breely said with a sob. "Who would do this?"

"I can give you a ride to your home." Her rescuer checked his cell phone. "I have to leave when I get a phone call from the hospital."

"Why would you get a phone call from the hospital?" she asked. "Are you sick?"

He shook his head. "No, I'm scheduled to transport organs to Denver. I have to leave when they call. The sooner the cases are delivered, the better."

"You don't have to take me home," Breely said. "I can call for a taxi, or Stan can take me."

"I can take Bea to her apartment," Stan said from behind Breely.

The flirt shook his head. "I'll take her home," he said.

Breely stood with her cheek to his chest, wondering if she'd lost her mind by allowing the man to drive her anywhere when she didn't know much about him. Her fingers curled into his shirt. "Who are you?"

He chuckled. "That's right. We haven't been properly introduced." He leaned back and stared down into her eyes, his own eyes as black as the night around them. "I'm Morris Cleveland. Most people call me Moe."

"Bea, I don't mind taking you to your place," Stan insisted. "What do you know about this guy, anyway?"

"He saved my life." She shook her head. "But thank you, Stan. You need to get home to your wife and family. I want...Moe...to take me."

Stan cut a narrow-eyed stare at Moe. "Hurt her, and you'll regret it."

Moe nodded. "Roger."

To Breely, Stan said, "I'll get a tow truck out in the morning to tow your car to a tire shop."

"Thank you, Stan." Breely knew she should move out of Moe's embrace. The full-body quakes had subsided into trembling. But she couldn't make herself move. Moe felt...safe.

"We need to get moving if I'm to get you to your place and back to the hospital before they need me there," Moe said. "Ready?"

She drew in a deep, steadying breath. "I will be as soon as I grab my bag from inside."

Moe shot one more glance in Stan's direction. "I'll take good care of her."

"Do that," Stan said. "And, Bea, let me know if I need to find a replacement for you this weekend. I'll understand."

She nodded. "Thank you."

Bea led Moe through the back door to the storage room, where several old school lockers lined one wall. She reached inside one and grabbed a large handbag and a puffy jacket. "I'm ready."

Moe hooked her arm and exited through the back door.

Stan nodded to Bea from where he stood with the sheriff.

Moe led Bea around to the front of the building to an SUV with the Bozeman Yellowstone International Airport logo emblazoned on the doors. "It's a loaner while I'm in town," he explained as he opened the passenger door.

Bea placed her bag and jacket on the floorboard. Moe helped her into her seat.

When she fumbled to secure her seatbelt, he leaned across and snapped it in place.

His face was so close that all she had to do was lean forward just a bit and her lips would touch his stubbled chin.

Her pulse quickened, and her breaths caught and held in her chest at the exact point where his shirt brushed against hers.

He turned to face her. "Are you okay?" He touched a finger to the base of her throat. "Your pulse is still pounding. I can see it. You should have let the EMT take you to the hospital for a complete exam."

"I'm okay," she whispered, afraid to drag in enough air to expand her lungs and raise her breasts to touch more than fabric against him.

He stared a moment longer, his eyebrows forming a V over his nose. "I'm not convinced."

Finally, he pulled out of the vehicle, closed the door and rounded the front to climb into the driver's seat. He started the engine and sat with his hand on the shift, his gaze moving to Breely, a crooked grin widening his lips.

"What?" Breely asked. "Is everything all right? Did you change your mind? You are under no obligation to ferry me around."

He pressed a finger to his lips. "Shh. It's okay. I'm taking you home. But to do that, I need to know where you live."

Breely's cheeks heated. She let go of the breath she'd been holding and laughed. "I guess it would help to know." She gave him the address.

He entered the data into the map application on his cell phone. When he was done, he showed her the screen. "Is that it?"

Leaning over the console, she nodded. "That's it." She sat back against the seat, staring out at the streets lined with lights at each corner.

He could take her anywhere, and no one would find her.

"Relax. I'm not going to abduct you," Moe said. "If I were, I would be wearing a ski mask like the jerks who grabbed you. Stan's seen my face and probably watched as we drove away, memorizing the license plate on this vehicle."

She gave him a weak smile. "Sorry. I'm a bit punchy. It's not every day I'm grabbed, knocked silly and thrown into a van."

"Nothing to be sorry about. You are the victim. I just wish I'd been able to hold onto at least one of those bastards. I should've hit them harder." He took one hand off the steering wheel and absently rubbed the knuckles of the other as he came to a stop at a traffic light.

"What bothers me is why they grabbed you in the first place. If they're looking to add you to a human trafficking ring, you'd bring a high price with that hair." He glanced her way, his lips turning upward in a wry grin.

"All the more reason to dye my hair dirt brown. Or, better yet, cotton candy pink."

"It's your hair. You can dye it any color you want." He shot a glance at her. "Me, personally, I like its natural color."

"Thank you." Breely glanced his way. "My grandmother had red hair like mine. She let me brush it when I was a little girl. It already had gray streaks in it. By the time she turned seventy, it was a stunning shade of white. When I'm seventy, I hope my hair is that exact same shade."

"And you'll still have sexy hair," he said, still grinning.

The heat returned to her cheeks, making them burn. Breely pressed her cool palms to her skin, refusing to look at Moe the Flirt.

He turned onto the street with her apartment building and drove into the parking lot, coming to a stop.

Breely quickly opened her door. "Thank you for

bringing me home." She dropped to the ground and hurried toward the front entry. When Breely reached for the door handle, her fingers were brushed gently to the side.

Moe's strong, capable fingers wrapped around the knob and pulled the door open.

Breely led the way up a set of stairs and down a long hallway to stop at her door. When she started to shove her key into the lock, barely applying any pressure, the door swung open. The doorjamb and the door itself were splintered.

Breely automatically recoiled backward several steps. "I locked it this morning," she whispered.

"Locks don't always work against crowbars. Get out your cell phone," he commanded as he bent to pull a knife out of a scabbard strapped to his ankle. "Call 911."

Breely keyed the numbers to place the call.

She had just punched the send button when Moe leaned close and said, "Stay here."

Breely's heart leaped into her throat. "What are you going to do?"

"If someone is in there, I'm not waiting for him to get out and run."

She didn't have time to respond as the dispatcher came on.

With Moe entering a potentially dangerous situation and a dispatcher in her ear, Breely fought the urge to race in after him. Instead, she relayed the information about the break-in at her apartment.

Once she had given the address and was assured a unit was on the way, Breely ended the call, pushed the door open wider and gasped.

CHAPTER 3

MOE MOVED QUICKLY and silently through the apartment, his knife held in front of him, his ears straining for the slightest sounds.

Whoever had been, or was still, in Bea's apartment had trashed everything so completely that Moe doubted anything could be salvaged.

Couch seat cushions had been ripped down the middle as if someone with a knife as sharp as Moe's had stabbed the fabric and the foam inside several times. The back and frame had suffered a similar attack.

Side tables lay in splintered pieces across the living room floor, and the glass coffee table was nothing more than shards strewn across the once cream-colored carpet.

Plants lay on their sides, the pots upended and black soil ground into the rug.

The damage was regretful but didn't occupy Moe's consciousness as much as searching for danger and neutralizing it before it neutralized him or Bea.

A thorough search of the living room, kitchen, pantry and coat closets yielded the usual items found in such places; only all had been consigned to the walls or floors. Bags of flour and sugar had been punctured, their contents spewed like a dusting of snow and ice crystals across counters and floors.

Nobody lurked in the dark places at the front of the apartment.

Moe slipped deeper into the disaster, turning down a short hallway. A door on the right hung open, leading into a bathroom. A white shower curtain hung in tatters, gaping holes slashed through the fabric, the curtain rod bent almost in half, dangling from one mount on the wall. Shampoo and cleaning fluids made the floor slick.

Small plastic containers of makeup lay crushed amid the pools of liquid. No one hid behind what was left of the shower curtain or in the tight confines of the linen cabinet.

Passing through to the bedroom, Moe quickly checked the closet and beneath what was left of the bed, the mattress hanging half off the frame with multiple stab wounds down the center.

After a quick check through the French doors onto the minuscule balcony, Moe turned and hurried back to Bea.

He found her kneeling among the shattered remains of the living room side tables, picking up the pieces of a torn photograph.

Bea's hands shook. The only spots of color on her pale face were the rusty freckles scattered across her nose, her green eyes and the shadowy crescents beneath them.

She stood, clutching the tiny fragments of paper in her fist. "Who would do this?" Her voice caught. The muscles in her throat convulsed as she swallowed hard. "And why?"

Fear and desolation etched lines across her forehead and deepened the dark shadows beneath her eyes.

His heart pinching hard in his chest, Moe gathered her into his arms. "These are just things. What's important is that you weren't here when whoever did this was."

She leaned her forehead into his shirt and shivered violently. "I've never been afraid of anything in my life." Her fingers curled into his shirt. "Until now," she whispered. Bea looked up into his eyes. "How do people live like this?"

He brushed a strand of her ginger hair off her forehead. "Fear isn't a bad thing. It makes you more aware of your surroundings and reminds you that you can be brave in the face of it."

"Were you afraid in the war?" she asked

He smiled crookedly. "Every damn day."

Her brow crinkled. "What did you do?"

"I used that fear. It gave me laser focus and helped me see clearly exactly what I had to do. I powered through. I didn't let it beat me."

She looked down at the shredded bits of a photograph. "They're just things," she echoed and let the bits of paper filter through her fingers like confetti. When she looked around at the destruction, she shook her head. "How can I stay in this apartment? The locks on the door did nothing to keep them out."

"Sweetheart, you can't stay in this apartment or this town. Not alone, anyway." His hand tightened slightly at the small of her back. "You need to be somewhere safe, with someone looking out for you."

Her brow furrowed. "I don't need a babysitter. I'm a grown woman, capable of defending myself. I've taken several self-defense classes. Hell, I'm a black belt in Tae Kwon Do." Her lips twisted. "And it didn't do me a whole lot of good when two men ganged up on me." Her eyes widened. "I have a gun." She stepped away from Moe's embrace and ducked into the bedroom.

Moe followed.

Bea jerked open the nightstand drawer and swore a stream of curses that would make a sailor blush. "I *had* a gun. The bastard took it."

"One thing is certain," Moe declared. "You can't stay here."

"I have to." Bea glanced around at the mess. "I don't have anywhere else to go."

"Don't you have family you can stay with?" Moe asked.

Bea's brow dipped lower. "Absolutely not."

Moe stared at the woman, trying to decipher what she meant by *absolutely not*. She'd spoken the two words with such vehemence they had to mean something to her.

"What about a friend?" he asked.

She shook her head, a small smile playing on her lips. "I told you I had high hopes you might be one of my first friends in the Bozeman area. You quickly squashed my chances since you're not staying."

Moe's cell phone vibrated in his back pocket. He pulled it out, stared down at the screen, swore and looked up to meet her gaze. "It's the hospital. They'll have my package ready in fifteen minutes. I need to get there quickly, then fly to Denver with the transportable organs."

"Yes, you do." Bea looked around at the mess. "Leave me here to manage the police. Go. Save lives." She gripped his arm and turned him toward the door. "Seriously, I'll be fine."

Moe dug in his heels. "You're not staying here." He turned, took her hand and stared into her eyes. "Do you trust me?"

Her brow twisted. "As much as I trust a man I met less than two hours ago who just happened to save my life." She shrugged. "So far, you haven't done anything to make me *dis*trust you."

He chuckled. "I hope I never do." His hand tightened around hers. "I don't have time to discuss this or argue. Lives are at stake. Yours and the people who will benefit from those organs."

"I don't know where you're going with this. What are you trying to say?"

He sighed. "I need to leave right now."

"I understand." She lifted her chin and squared her shoulders. "You're not responsible for me. I can take care of myself."

"Like you did with the two goons and the van?" He shook his head. "I don't have time to come up with a better idea than this..." He tucked her hand in the crook of his arm. "Come with me." Moe marched her toward the door.

She let him lead her through the apartment and out into the hallway before she ground to a halt. "You have organs to deliver. You don't have time to find me a hotel or a friend for me to stay with."

"I know." He started walking again, pulling her along. "You're coming with me."

She trotted alongside him a few more steps, her frown deepening. "Where are you going to drop me? The hospital or a police station?"

He shook his head and kept moving, leading her down the stairs and out into the parking lot. "I'm not dropping you anywhere." Moe yanked open the passenger door, helped her into the SUV and buckled her seatbelt. "I'm taking you with me to Denver."

"What?" she cried as he shut the door.

He had to get to the hospital, receive the organs and move on to the plane. He didn't have time to find someone to watch over the pretty red-haired waitress. He slid into the driver's seat and started the engine.

Before Moe could pull out of the parking lot, Bea fumbled with her seatbelt. "Let me out here. I'll call Stan and have him pick me up. He'll let me stay with him and his family."

"Come to think about it, you can't stay with your boss or friends. It won't work. Not with the way things played out tonight." Moe covered her hand still struggling with the seatbelt. He briefly pinned her gaze with a steady one of his own. "What's Stan's background?"

Bea tried to peel his hand off hers. "You know him. He owns the Tumbleweed Tavern."

"Prior military?" Moe asked.

The redhead shrugged. "I don't know. He's never talked about being in the military."

Moe released her hand and shifted into drive, pulling out of the parking lot onto the street. "Has he ever been in law enforcement or worked as a bodyguard?"

She quit trying to release the belt buckle. "I think he was a bouncer before he bought the tavern."

"Do you expect Stan to protect you?"

"Not really." Her lips thinned into a straight line. "But isn't there safety in numbers?"

"Do they have children?" Moe drove toward the hospital.

"Yes. A five-year-old boy and a teenage girl." Bea crossed her arms over her chest. "Could you get to the point?"

"Stan isn't trained to protect or fight, other than breaking up a barroom brawl or two. Someone made a play for you tonight and trashed your apartment." Moe kept driving, his foot heavy on the accelerator. "If you stay at Stan's house, and the people who are after you decide to try again—"

Bea sighed. "I'll put Stan and his family at risk."

"Trying to get to you could make that little boy, the teenage girl, their mother *and* your boss collateral damage." He shot a glance in her direction. "Is that what you want?"

She shook her head and dropped her hands into her lap. Bea stared straight ahead as her brow puckered. "You think they'll make another attempt to kidnap me?" she asked, her voice wavering.

Moe didn't like scaring the woman who'd already had the fright of her life that evening, but he had a job to do. Knowing she would be okay would help him get that job done quickly.

"Look," he said in as calm a voice as he could. "I can't leave you alone. I won't leave you alone. For some reason, you have a target pinned on your back. Until I complete my first mission, I can't concentrate on resolving your issue."

She nodded. "Getting those organs to Denver is more important than finding a babysitter for me. Those organs represent hope for several people. Not one lone waitress."

Moe held tightly to the steering wheel with his left hand and reached across the console with his right hand, capturing her fingers in his. "Your life is no less important."

She snorted. "How do you know? A kidney might save the life of a father with small children. Eyes might give a mother her sight back so she can see her baby's first smile. I'm neither a father or mother of small children nor the sole caretaker of an elderly parent. No one is relying on me." She nodded. "I don't want to delay critical assets from the people who need them most."

As Moe approached the hospital, he slowed and followed the emergency room signs. Several people emerged from the building dressed in scrubs. One held what appeared to be a medium-sized cooler in his hands.

Moe shifted into park and stepped out of the borrowed SUV.

Within less than a couple of minutes, the team had the documentation scanned and instructions relayed. The man holding the cooler settled it on the backseat floorboard.

As soon as the container was secure, Moe hopped into the SUV and drove to the airport with Bea sitting silently in the seat beside him. He wondered what was going through her head but didn't have time to worry about her when his first priority was the precious cargo he'd been entrusted with.

He parked at the Fixed Base Operator building that serviced the general aviation needs of the airport, hopped out and grabbed the container from the back floorboard.

Bea met him at the door to the building and hurried to keep up with him as he passed through the building, waved at the desk clerk and stepped out onto the tarmac.

He'd had the fuel topped off before he'd left the airport earlier. All he had to do was perform his preflight check and quickly file the flight plan he'd preloaded earlier.

Within minutes, he'd stowed the cargo in the cabin, completed his preflight check and handed Bea up into the plane. Once seated, he passed a headset to Bea and slipped his over his ears. "Buckle up. They'll have us moving before you know it."

Moments later, Ground Control had them taxiing to the end of the runway. When Moe received permission to take off, he eased the throttle forward, sending the little plane racing down the runway. Their speed inched upward until they were going fast enough to take off. Moe eased back on the yoke, and the aircraft lifted off the ground.

Once the Air Traffic Controller vectored them onto a southern trajectory, Moe drew a deep breath and let it out slowly. He glanced back at the box he'd strapped into the seat harness. Finally, he glanced at Bea. "Hanging in there?" he said into his mic.

She nodded, her lips moving, though he couldn't hear her. He reached across and adjusted her mic to fit in front of her mouth, his knuckles brushing her soft lips. A shock of electricity ricocheted across his nerve endings. He jerked back his hand as if it had been scalded and returned his attention to the instrument panel and the sky around him. "Talk to me," he said.

"Can you hear me now?" she asked, her voice even sexier over the radio. How was that even possible?

"I hear you," he said. "You might as well sit back and relax. Take a nap if you want. We'll be in the air for a couple of hours."

Bea turned a little in her seat. She didn't appear too worried about being in a small plane.

Moe could feel her gaze on him without even looking in her direction. "Have you been up in a small airplane?"

"I have."

He looked. "Oh, yeah? What kind?"

"I'd like to say I know something about airplanes,

41

but the truth is I know next to nothing. Other than they have wings and fly."

His lips twitched. "Was it the same size as this plane?"

She frowned. "Bigger. It had ten seats, not counting the pilot and copilot."

"A much more expensive plane," Moe commented. "Had your business chartered it for an event?"

She shook her head, staring out the window. "No, they owned it."

"Nice."

Bea shrugged. "Some think owning more property will make them happy. But owning property means being owned by your responsibilities toward that property or corporation. You get so busy you forget you have a life outside the entity until your child is grown and gone and all you have left is a corporation and no family." Bea gave him a wan smile. "Sorry. That was too deep for a flight through the stars." She gazed out the window and sighed. "The sky is amazing up here, away from light pollution and the noise of cars and trucks rumbling by."

"We rarely have bumper-to-bumper traffic out here," Moe said. "I like that I don't get road rage, and I can land almost anywhere. It's a great way to travel."

"Do you fly for any commercial airlines?" Bea asked.

"No. I'm not interested in driving a glorified bus or arguing over who got the chicken cordon bleu and who got the veggie plate. I fly to get myself to different places, but mostly because I love it. What about you? Why would someone try to kidnap you and then trash your place? It's not like a random occurrence. They knew you got off work at that time. They also had to know when you wouldn't be home and how long, giving them plenty of time to destroy your home."

She stared straight ahead, her jaw tight, her lips pressed into a thin line. "All I wanted was to live a normal life, like everyone else in the world."

His hands tightened on the yoke. "What do you mean?"

She looked down at her hands in her lap. "I thought that if I could start over somewhere no one knew me, I might actually have a chance at living the way I want to live, not having my life mapped out for me by someone else or being chased by the media." She turned toward him with a watery smile. "And it was working. For a few short weeks, I was Bea Smith, a waitress at the Tumbleweed Tavern in Bozeman. I was paying my own rent on an apartment I furnished with thrift shop finds on my tip money."

Moe shook his head slowly. "Wait. Let me get this straight… You're not Bea, the waitress?"

"Yes, and no." She looked out at the stars. "Yes. I'm the waitress who served you and others at the tavern. I'm also the only living child of my parents, and when they're gone, I'll inherit a multi-billion-dollar global corporation I never wanted."

"Sweet Jesus," Moe muttered under his breath. "Who the hell are you?"

Bea sighed. "This is the part where I tell you, and things get all weird."

"As long as I don't get hit with kidnapping charges, I'm good. As far as I'm concerned, we all put our pants on the same way. How much money you have in your wallet doesn't make you a better or worse person."

Her lips twisted. "You say that now, but you'd be surprised how it changes how people look at you."

His curiosity was piqued, but Moe didn't pressure her to reveal her real name. She'd been through a lot that day. The last thing she needed was someone demanding to know her well-guarded secret.

"Can I just stay Bea Smith, the waitress at Tumbleweed Tavern?" she asked with a wistful sigh.

"You can be anyone you want. Unfortunately, your secret isn't secret anymore. If you're the only heir to a huge fortune, that would explain why someone would want to kidnap you." He frowned. "It doesn't explain why someone would trash your apartment. Did you have some proprietary documents or items that were worth stealing stored in your place?"

Bea shook her head. "No. I left it all behind. I still work for my father's philanthropic foundation, but that's all online. I carry my laptop with me in case I need to log in." She patted the oversized purse she'd carried aboard.

Moe's glance settled on the bag containing the laptop. "Could you have data on your laptop they might be after?"

She shook her head. "I only tap into the philanthropy database. Not the corporation's information."

"Trashing your apartment doesn't make sense if they weren't looking for something." He tapped his thumb on the yoke. "Did you make someone mad? Someone who would want to harm or scare you?"

Bea shrugged. "There's always those quick to blame my family or the corporation for everything wrong in their lives, real or imagined. It's possible."

"The thing is, *your* apartment was trashed. Not your parents' place," Moe pointed out.

"They have a state-of-the-art security system on the ranch," Bea said. "No one can get in or out without triggering alarms or being captured on camera."

"Can you think of anyone, in particular, you might have inadvertently snubbed? Rejected? Fired?"

"Not since I've been out on my own. There has been the occasional customer who can't keep his hands to himself." She smiled. "Stan takes care of them."

"Why didn't you tell the sheriff who you were?

That kind of information will help them in the kidnapping investigation."

Bea shrugged. "I didn't want it to get back to my folks. They'll flip out and insist I move back to the ranch."

"Is that such a bad idea?" Moe asked.

Her face hardened. "I can't live with them. They would cocoon me in bubble wrap and make me a prisoner in their home to keep from losing me."

"Sounds like they love you," Moe observed.

She snorted. "I could do with a lot less of that kind of love. I want to live, to feel and experience the world around me, more than the ranch near Kalispell."

"That's a beautiful part of Montana," Moe observed.

Bea held up her hands. "Don't get me wrong. I love the ranch. It was a great place to grow up. To me, there's more to life than just staying alive. Not to my parents. After losing their only son, my older brother, to leukemia, they fixated on me. I couldn't step outside without a helmet. Couldn't breathe without them fearing I would catch some fatal virus." She laughed without humor. "They insisted on homeschooling me and that I attend college online rather than going in person. I'm almost thirty, and I've barely been outside Montana. We went on vacation a couple of times, but my mother and father were so worried about me that they didn't enjoy the time away from the ranch. I had to escape. I didn't tell my parents where I'd gone. I escaped." She lifted her chin and stared across at Moe. "I can't go back."

"They must love you a great deal," Moe offered.

"They do," she said, "and I love them, too. That's why it took me so long to leave. I saw how broken-hearted they were when my brother Ryan died. I didn't have the heart to rebel against them hovering over me." She turned away to stare out the window to her right, unaware of how her sad expression reflected in the glass. "I'm twenty-eight years old, and I've never been on a date. I didn't have any friends. I've never left Montana. I had to leave."

"You didn't get outside of Montana," Moe pointed out.

Her crooked smile touched his heart. "One step at a time. I needed to prove that I could support myself. I didn't want to tap into my bank account or use credit cards that could reveal my location. Thankfully, I had enough cash to tide me over for a few days until I found the job at the tavern. The tips were good enough to cover the rent on my apartment and groceries.

"I couldn't leave the family philanthropies hanging, so I work during the weekdays managing them online. My mother and father can see me there."

"Can't they trace you through your computer location?" he asked.

She smiled. "I have a friend who can mask my IP

address by sending it all over the world. A really talented hacker might be able to trace me back to Bozeman, though I had hoped not."

"You need to let the Bozeman police and county sheriff know your true identity. Otherwise, they'll chase the wrong leads and waste time and resources."

Bea sighed. "Yeah. I know you're right. It means I'll have to relocate to another town."

"Relocating might not be enough," Moe said. "If they found you once, there's a good chance they'll do it again."

"That's what I'm afraid of." Bea looked straight ahead. "That's one of the disadvantages of being the daughter of one of the richest men in the world."

Moe's gut clenched. "How rich is your father?"

Bea turned to him, met and held his gaze. "Ever heard of Robert Brantt?"

Moe's eyes widened. "*The* Robert Brantt of Brantt Enterprises?"

Bea's lips twisted. "So, you've heard of him."

"Who hasn't?" Moe blinked.

Bea reached out her hand.

Moe automatically took it and shook it.

"I'm Breely Brantt," she said. "Robert and Fiona Brantt's only living child."

Moe let out a long, low whistle. "Yeah. You definitely need to let the detectives working your case in on your secret. I suspect your true identity has everything to do with the kidnapping and trashing of your apartment."

"Unfortunately," Breely said, "like you pointed out, you could become collateral damage if you stay with me long enough."

"Don't worry about me. I'll take my chances." He glanced back at the box containing the organs he'd promised to deliver. "After we transfer the cargo, I'll want to put in a call to my boss, Hank Patterson. I'm sure he'll want to know what's going on."

She frowned. "Why?"

Moe met her gaze with a steady one of his own. "What he does...what we do...is exactly what you need."

"And what is that?"

"Not what, but who." Moe grinned. "I'm a member of a group of former military special forces operatives called Brotherhood Protectors. Hank Patterson's brainchild. We provide protection, rescue and extraction services to those in need. Sweetheart, I'd say you're in need."

Her brow dipped. "No offense, but it sounds like a bunch of glorified bodyguards." Breely's head shifted from side to side. "No thanks."

"Not even close," Moe said. "Every one of us is highly trained in combat, intelligence, explosives and maneuvering in dangerous and difficult places. Hank only hires the best of the best."

"The last thing I need is a bodyguard who thinks

too highly of himself." She leaned her head back and closed her eyes. "I'm trying to get away from a lifetime of constraints. If I'm saddled with a bodyguard, someone I don't know or care to know, I might as well move back to the ranch my father has built into a fortress."

Moe reached for her hand. "I'd volunteer for this mission myself," he said. "You already know me."

Her gaze went to where his hand held hers. "You'd do that?"

He nodded. "I would."

"It wouldn't bother you to babysit the poor little rich girl?"

"I never let rank or the status of a person's bank account affect the way I treat them. You're just another person who needs a little help to stay alive."

"Key word..."

"Alive."

Her frown remained, along with her hand in his. "I'll think about it."

"Good. You have a few minutes left before we land. Then I'll need your decision. Whether you go with us or someone else, you can't wander around alone. Unless you're looking for a way to die."

CHAPTER 4

BREELY SAT BACK in her seat, feeling a little weight lift off her chest. Running away from home at twenty-eight years old might have seemed silly to anyone else.

To her, it had been terrifying. She'd grown up sheltered to the point of living in a very tight cocoon. The freedom of being her own person without having to answer to anyone had been heady and welcome.

She'd learned a lot about freedom she hadn't real-ized before.

Foremost, she'd learned a person was never truly free. She had to answer to others no matter what she did. As a waitress, she'd had to answer to her boss, the customers and herself.

Doing what was right wasn't always easy. Living out from under her parents' oppressive desire to keep her safe wasn't the answer. Running away might not have been the right answer. All she knew was that she needed to make her own decisions. Live her own life.

But, after nearly being kidnapped, maybe she needed a little help to keep from costing her father a huge ransom. She knew he'd pay it.

It chapped her ass that she had to have help. As long as her parents were billionaires, she'd be a target. Her father would have to publicly relinquish every last cent and control of his many corporations before his family was free. She'd been kidding herself to think she might escape the noose of wealth. "I just want to blend into society, to be a regular Joe."

Moe smiled. "You could never be a regular Joe. And Breely suits you and your flaming hair."

She lifted a hand to her curls. "I should dye it. I'm sure it's not helping me stay hidden from kidnappers and the paparazzi." Memories flooded her thoughts. "Ever since I spent time with my grandmother, who had the same red hair, I've been proud of my legacy. Now..." She pulled on a strand. "Maybe I should shave it off. Anything to make myself invisible."

"Shaving off your hair will make you stand out even more than the red hair." Moe's gaze swept over head and face. "Don't do it. Your hair is beautiful."

Though her chest and cheeks warmed at the compliment, Breely shook her head. "If I don't shave it off or dye it pink, I need to buy a wig or hat and keep it covered. It's a dead giveaway."

"If you must hide it for the short term, a hat can be easily undone. More so than pink dye or a buzz cut." He glanced at the map on the control panel. "We'll be landing soon. I have a hat stashed in the back of your seat. Transporting organs can sometimes involve journalists looking for a story on a slow-news night."

"Seriously?" Breely shook her head.

"Catching a photo of a multi-billionaire's daughter stepping off a plane in Denver might be considered more newsworthy than saving lives with organ transplants."

"Sadly, true," Breely agreed. She unbuckled her seat harness and got up on her knees in her seat to reach into the pocket on the back.

Moe received instructions from Denver ATC to establish a flight path for landing at the Denver International Airport.

Breely had her hand in the seat's pocket, looking for the hat Moe had offered when the plane suddenly lurched and dropped.

Thrown off balance, Breely tipped sideways and fell into Moe's lap, hitting the yoke and sending the plane sideways.

When she tried to get up out of Moe's way, he ordered, "Stay still until I right the plane." With one hand on her ass, Moe pulled her hip away from the yoke, pressing her body firmly against his. Then he extricated his other arm from beneath her, grabbed the yoke and eased the plane back on course.

Breely's heart pounded against her ribs. Cradled in Moe's arms, her breasts smashed to his chest, her cheek pressed to his neck, and she couldn't decide if it was fear or desire making her breathing and pulse erratic. "I'm sorry."

He chuckled. "Can't say that I am." He winked. "I've never flown with a beautiful woman draped across my lap."

Knowing she should move back to her seat, she hesitated, loving how warm and solid he was. The man wasn't a hulking, muscle-bound guy. What he was, however, was compact, wiry and strong, based on how he held her entire body tightly against his with only one arm.

The Denver ATC jolted Breely out of her lusty stupor, giving Moe instructions to turn and establish his flight path to a runway.

His mouth twitched. "Much as I like this, I need both hands to land."

"Right. I'll just…" Breely pushed her hand against his thigh, her fingertips brushing against the hard ridge beneath the fly of his jeans. Her breath caught.

"Told you I liked it," he murmured as he helped her off his lap and back into her seat. "Buckle up, Buttercup. We're going in for the landing." He reached behind her seat, fished out a Denver Broncos ball cap and handed it to her.

While Moe focused solely on landing the plane, Breely twisted her hair up into a bun, secured it with an elastic band and shoved it all up into the ball cap before pulling the bill down low on her forehead.

She'd never been in the co-pilot seat of one of her father's airplanes and found it both exhilarating and terrifying to witness the landing. A crosswind made it even more challenging. The wings tipped, and the aircraft seemed to wobble as they hurtled toward the tarmac.

Breely pressed her feet into the floor as if she could slow their descent by pressing on imaginary brakes.

When Breely thought they would surely crash onto the runway, Moe eased back on the yoke and the small plane kissed the tarmac, landing with a soft bump. They rolled halfway down the runway until he turned off onto a taxiway and stopped in front of a building where an ambulance waited with people standing beside it.

Breely finally remembered to breathe. "That was amazing."

Moe chuckled. "Thank you. Were you worried?"

She nodded. "The ground seemed to be rising up to meet us, we were going so fast."

"It is a little disconcerting when you're learning

how to fly, but it becomes second nature the more you do it."

She pressed a hand to her chest. "I'll have to believe you. I'll never learn to fly."

"Never say never," he said with a grin. "You might want to stay inside while I make the transfer."

"Good idea." Breely pulled the bill of the hat down lower over her brow and remained in her seat.

Moe pulled the plane to a halt and switched off the engine. While the propeller blades slowed to a stop, Moe unbuckled his seatbelt and climbed into the back of the plane to retrieve the precious cargo.

With the container in his hands, he stepped down from the plane and met the medical personnel there to transport the organs to their destination.

After the tag was scanned and the medical staff had signed for the container, the organs were loaded into the ambulance.

The gate opened, and the ambulance left the airport, engaging the emergency lights to get to the hospital faster.

Moe stepped up into the aircraft. "You can come out now." He held out his hand to help her disembark.

Once on the ground, she slipped her arms into her jacket, looped her purse over her shoulder and stared at the disappearing ambulance lights. "I hope all goes well with the transplants." Those people really were getting a fresh start in life. It made her feel proud to have been on the flight that delivered so much hope. "You've done a good thing," she said softly.

"I'm glad to do it."

Out of the corner of her eye, she could see him watching the ambulance disappear around a corner.

Breely turned and looked up at him. "What now?"

He faced her. "It's getting late. I hadn't planned on flying back to Bozeman tonight. Besides, we don't know where your kidnappers are or if they'll make another attempt. I doubt they've secured a flight to Denver on short notice unless they have access to a private plane. You're better off staying in Denver for the night. It will give you a chance to think about your next move."

She nodded. "I should have enough cash in my purse for a hotel room."

"I made a reservation for a rental car and a hotel room downtown. You can come with me."

She smiled. "Seeing as I don't have a car waiting for me, I'd appreciate the ride."

He dipped his head. "My pleasure." Moe reached inside the plane, grabbed a backpack and slung it over one shoulder. He closed and locked the door to the aircraft and led the way into the building.

A dark-haired woman at the counter stood as they approached. "Mr. Cleveland, your rental car is in the parking lot." She handed him a set of keys.

He gave the clerk a smile that melted Breely's knees. "Thank you," he said.

The brunette's cheeks flushed a soft shade of pink. Apparently, Moe's smile had the same effect on the woman as it had on Breely.

"Do you want us to top off your fuel?" she asked. Was she really batting her eyes at the man?

"Yes, please," he said. "We'll be leaving around ten o'clock tomorrow morning."

"I'll have them fill it up tonight in case you decide to leave earlier. I made the reservation for your hotel. It's a good thing you requested a room ahead of time. There's a Broncos game in town as well as a big concert. The hotels were filling up fast." She handed him a printout of the hotel room reservation.

Again, he smiled, charm oozing from his handsome face. "Thank you for taking care of the arrangements."

Breely had been the recipient of that same smile at the tavern. The man had a way of making a woman feel like she was the only person in the room. Seeing that magic work on someone else had butterflies storming inside her belly, at the same time as it made her want to claw the other woman's eyes out.

That thought made her blink and take a step backward. Where the hell had that come from? She'd never been jealous of another woman. Envious, yes. Jealous?

Moe wasn't her man. She'd just met him that evening.

The only relationship experience Breely had with a man had been limited to a brief clandestine fling with one of the young cowboys on her father's ranch.

She'd fancied herself in love with the man. But after a few awkward romps in the hay—which she wouldn't recommend to anyone—she'd lost her virginity and hadn't thought much of sex. On more than one occasion, she'd wondered if all the hype about making love was just that...hype. For her, it had been painful the first time and uncomfortable the others.

Though her cowboy had seemed to like it at the time, it hadn't been enough to keep him there. He'd disappeared to go to work at a ranch in Texas, claiming Montana was far too cold. Looking back, Breely wondered if her father had had anything to do with the man's decision to leave.

Had she really loved the cowboy and he loved her, Breely might have gone with him. However, he hadn't declared his love at any point in their time together, and she'd promised herself that she wouldn't declare herself until he had. After a few weeks, Breely had gotten over him and was lonelier than ever.

Surrounded by her family, the housekeeper, cook and ranch staff, she'd been alone and craving a chance to explore the world and people outside the Rocky Ridge Ranch.

"Ready?" Moe asked.

Breely had been so caught up in the rush of memories she hadn't realized Moe was now facing her with humor tugging at the corners of his lips.

She nodded, heat rising up her neck into her cheeks. "I am."

Moe led the way out of the building to a parking lot. He hit the unlock button on the key fob, and lights flashed from a black SUV. Moe opened the passenger door and handed Breely into the seat.

His hand on her arm sent electric shocks blasting through her body and heat simmering low in her belly.

She'd felt something similar, if not as intense when she'd been with the cowboy.

Moe settled in the driver's seat, keyed the address into his cell phone's map application and connected his phone to the vehicle. After buckling his seatbelt, he started the engine and left the airport.

A clear sky allowed the stars overhead to light the landscape. On the outskirts of the city, Denver's airport was surrounded by flat, dry land. Breely would consider it a desert. City lights glowed to the west of the airport, and beyond them was the ghostly glow of snow-capped peaks.

They were as beautiful from the ground as they'd been from the sky, flying into the airport.

Breely sat forward in her seat, eager to take it all in. A different city in a state other than Montana... She sighed, a smile automatically curling her lips.

Moe chuckled. "I take it you've never been to Denver."

"Never," she admitted. "I've seen so many places on the television or the internet, but I've only visited a few. The only time I left the ranch was to go to annual doctors' visits or a few family vacations."

"Where did you go on those vacations?"

"We went to a ranch in Canada, an exclusive resort in Hawaii and an island resort in the Bahamas. Each time, we were isolated from the locals, and the only people we came into contact with were members of the staff. We had our own pool, chef and stretch of beach." She stared at the city ahead. "When we were in the Bahamas, I remember hearing music from a nearby festival. I tried to sneak out and see what it was all about, but I set off the intruder alarm system on the grounds, and a dozen armed bodyguards converged on me." She laughed. "My father was mad." Breely shrugged. "I could deal with that, but my mother...she was shaking. The thought of her only child leaving the security of the resort made her physically ill. I didn't try to escape after that. I hated seeing her so worried."

"But you did escape to Bozeman," Moe pointed out.

Breely nodded. "Eleven years later. My mother

takes anti-anxiety medication now. And they know I'm okay because I've continued to manage my responsibilities relating to the Brantt philanthropies. I do video conferences with my staff and video interviews with the press. And I've emailed them every day since I left to let them know I'm doing well."

"How did they respond to your disappearance?" he asked.

"They weren't happy that I left. I think that because I didn't ghost them, they didn't send out a search party to find me."

"As close as you say they guarded you, I'm surprised they didn't launch an all-out missing persons alert."

She laughed. "I thought for sure my father would call out every law enforcement organization and the national guard. I left a note telling them I was leaving and not to do that. I guess the note helped."

"Do you miss them?" he asked.

Breely's chest tightened. "It's hard not to. After spending twenty-eight years with them, it was an adjustment to be on my own." She shook her head from side to side. "But I had to do it. I know it sounds cliché, but I needed to find myself."

"And have you?" Moe asked.

"I've only been out for two months. But I was getting there," she said. "As Bea Smith, working at the tavern, people didn't see me as the only child of Robert Brantt. They saw Bea, the waitress. It was liberating. Stan didn't treat me any differently than any other waitress." She glanced his way. "He's gruff but a big teddy bear with a soft heart. He gave me a job no one else would. I didn't have a resume or any job experience."

"Didn't you have to have a Social Security Number and a driver's license?"

"He paid me under the table. I think he knew I was on my last dollar, with no gas in my car and no food. I had just enough cash for my apartment deposit and first month's rent—which is more than a lot of homeless people have. If he hadn't given me the job, I would have had to beg for food and join the ranks of the homeless."

"Or go home," Moe said.

Breely's jaw hardened as she stared at the road ahead. "Not an option. It took a lot for me to leave. I wasn't going back until I went on my terms. For a visit. Not for good."

Moe turned off the interstate and headed into downtown Denver.

Excitement rippled through Breely as she stared up at the tall buildings. Though it was night, people walked along the streets. Couples held hands, passing beneath the softly glowing streetlights.

Moe pulled up to the front of their hotel, shifted into park and got out.

A valet stepped off the curb. "Checking in?"

"Yes, sir," Moe said.

The valet opened the passenger door and held it as Breely climbed out. Staring up at the marble columns and polished glass doors, she wished she was dressed more appropriately. The short denim skirt, midriff T-shirt advertising Tumbleweed Tavern and oversized puffy jacket didn't seem appropriate for the posh hotel. She looked more like a hooker than someone the establishment would want staying the night in their building.

When Moe joined her on the curb, Breely leaned close to him. "I'm not dressed for this place." She frowned. "And I doubt I have enough cash in my purse to stay a night here."

"Let's see what they have. If you need a bit more, I'll loan you the amount."

"I didn't leave my parents' home to rely on others to bail me out. Can you take me to a less expensive place?" She turned around in time to see the rental SUV being driven off by the valet. Her heart sank into her tennis shoes.

Moe hooked her arm. "Let's see what they have. Then, if you still want to leave, I can get them to bring the car around."

Too tired to argue, Breely let Moe escort her into the lobby, where they stood in a line of people checking in.

By the time the people in front of them made it to the reception desk, they were close enough to over-hear the clerk say, "I'm sorry, sir, we're fully booked.

I've called around to some of the hotels close by, and they're full as well. I even checked as far as the airport hotels. It's a big night in Denver. Every hotel I've called is at capacity."

The concierge stepped out from behind his desk and announced, "If you don't have a reservation, we're very sorry, but we don't have any rooms left."

"Not good." Breely looked around the lobby as several couples behind them left, grumbling. "Do you think they would frown if I slept on a couch in the lobby?"

"You're not sleeping in the lobby," he said, his voice a deep rumble.

"How about I sneak down to the garage and sleep in the back seat of the rental car?" She gave him a weak grin.

"It's supposed to get chilly tonight." He shook his head. "No. Let me get checked in, and we can come up with a plan."

The clerk gave a relieved sigh when Moe told him he had a reservation. Two minutes later, he had key cards in hand, a spare toiletries kit, and they were on their way up the elevator to the eleventh floor.

Tired, disheartened and sad that her first night in a city was going to be filled with trying to find cheap accommodations, Breely leaned against the wall while Moe touched the key card to the lock on the door. "I'll wait out here while you drop your backpack."

"I'm not leaving you out in the hall. You can wait inside." He pushed the door open and held it wide for her to enter ahead of him.

Breely met his gaze. "You do realize I've only known you for a few hours. It seems a stretch to walk into a hotel room with a stranger. How do I know you aren't going to take advantage of me?"

He let the door swing closed, his lips pressed into a thin line. "I'm tired and hungry." He took her hand in his, placed the key card in her palm and closed her fingers around it. "Take the room. I'll sleep out here in the hall or in the SUV. If I'd wanted to molest you, I've had several opportunities since I pulled your ass out of that van. I could've flown you to some remote location, raped you and left you for the wolves to find. But I didn't. The women I make love to come to me willingly or not at all. Besides, you're not my type."

Frowning, she tried to shove the card back at him. "I'm not taking your room. You made the reservation and paid for it. I'm not a charity case. I'll pay my way or sleep on a park bench with the other homeless people."

He refused to take the card and ran a hand through his hair. "Cut yourself some slack. You didn't ask to be attacked tonight. Come into the room, wash your face, comb your hair and use the facilities. Then we're going to find some food and make a plan."

"Do you know how tired I am of people telling me

what to do?" she whispered.

"Look, it's your choice. I'm going to walk away. You can choose to use that key or toss it and go sleep in a park with God knows who. Just remember, it'll be your choice. I'm going to find something to eat before I start slamming my fist into walls." He left her in front of the door and headed for the elevator.

Breely waited for him to turn and call his bluff.

Instead, he punched the button on the elevator. When the bell dinged and the door slid open, the man stepped in.

"Wait!" Breely called out and ran to catch up.

The doors were two inches from closing when she jammed her hand between them. They bounced open to reveal Moe leaning against the back wall, his arms folded, his legs crossed at the ankles and a frown creasing his forehead. "What?"

"Okay, you win." Breely held the doors open. "I'll use the room. I'll sleep on the chair or in the bathtub. You paid for the room. You get the bed."

His eyes narrowed. "It's your choice."

"Fine. It's my choice."

The elevator beeped a warning.

Still, Moe remained propped against the back wall. "I would never hurt you. I give you my word. And the only way I'd make love to you is if you asked me. Nicely. Then it would be my choice whether I agreed. Again...you're not my type. Understood?"

Breely nodded. "I'm not your type."

"And?" he prompted, unfazed by the loud beeping.

"And you won't hurt me or make love to me unless I ask. Which I won't." She cocked her eyebrow. "Now, are you coming out of that elevator before they send security up to find out why it's not moving?"

He hesitated a moment longer, then pushed away from the wall and walked toward her.

Breely stepped back, letting go of the elevator doors.

Moe walked through and allowed the doors to close behind him.

Breely let go of the breath she'd been holding.

When Moe held out his hand, she laid the key card in his palm. He walked ahead of her and opened the room door.

This time, he didn't hold the door for her but stepped through and let the door swing behind him.

Breely caught it before it closed and locked her out. She felt bad that she'd made him mad when all he'd done was try to help her.

But it was safer if he was mad. If she stayed the night in his hotel room, she'd be less tempted by his angry countenance than the charming one he'd displayed to the airport clerk earlier.

Hell, who was she kidding?

Even mad, the man had her knees weak and her panties damp.

It was going to be a long night.

CHAPTER 5

As tired as Moe was, he was hungry and needed to burn off the adrenaline that spiked as soon as he entered the hotel room and saw all the possibilities of a king-sized bed and a very small chair Breely couldn't possibly sleep on.

Holy hell.

He tossed his backpack on the desk and dug inside for his toothbrush, a comb and a fresh black T-shirt. He shot a glance at Breely, who stood looking out the window. He remembered how embarrassed she'd been standing outside the posh hotel, wearing the clothes she'd worn to work at the tavern.

"I have a clean T-shirt if you want to wear it instead of your work shirt," he said.

Breely turned, biting her bottom lip. "Are you sure you don't mind?"

"I wouldn't have offered if I did." He dug in the

backpack and pulled out another black T-shirt and tossed it her way.

She caught it and held it up in front of her.

Moe wasn't a big guy, but Breely was petite. The T-shirt would hang almost to her knees.

She smiled brightly. "Thanks."

"You can have the bathroom first," he said.

With a nod, she grabbed the spare toiletries kit and a brush from her purse. With the T-shirt over her shoulder, she ducked into the bathroom.

Moe crossed to the window and stared out at the Denver skyline and the streets below. He didn't much care for cities, preferring the wide-open spaces and mountains of Montana and Wyoming. Having grown up in the farmlands of South Dakota, the buildings packed close together and the crowds made him long to get back in the air, away from traffic, road rage and cranky people.

Standing where Breely had stood, looking down at the bright city lights, he could see the city from an entirely different perspective. Breely had been more or less a prisoner on a ranch in Montana all her life. Being the daughter of a very wealthy man hadn't been the perfect life everyone would have assumed. She'd probably never walked down a city street, smelled the variety of delicious foods available to enjoy or sat in a jazz club, listening to a band playing.

As late as it was, they'd have to settle for a bar and

grill. The restaurants would be closed, but the nightlife was just getting warmed up.

The bathroom door opened a lot sooner than he'd expected.

Moe turned as Breely stepped out, her red hair pulled up in a messy bun on top of her head with soft, loose curls cupping her chin. She'd traded the Tumbleweed T-shirt for his black one. With the sleeves rolled up to her shoulders and a knot tied in the hem that rested on her hip, she looked like a hip city girl ready for a night on the town.

"Is this okay?" she asked.

"My T-shirt never looked better."

Her cheeks flushed a soft pink. "Thanks."

Damn, she looked good. Her stubborn determination to be independent, coupled with her innate vulnerability, had Moe tied in knots. One minute he wanted to shake her; the next, he wanted to pull her into his arms and kiss that pretty mouth until she opened to him completely.

His pulse pounded through his veins, sending hot blood south where it had no business. He'd promised not to hurt her or make love to her unless she asked him to. And what were the chances of her asking him to make love to her when they'd only met a few hours ago?

He brushed past her. "I'll only be a minute." If his tone was a little gruff, good. Maybe she'd remain distant from him if he remained grumpy and angry.

It wouldn't be hard to do, considering the level of sexual frustration building steadily since they'd entered the hotel room.

He closed the door and drew in a deep breath. If he had time, he'd jump in a cold shower to shock his libido into submission.

His stomach grumbled. He hadn't eaten much at the tavern, preferring not to fly on a full stomach. Now, he was hungry, horny and needed something to distract him from the pretty redhead.

Moe stripped out of his shirt, ran cold water into the sink and splashed it on his face. It wasn't the icy shower he needed, but it would have to suffice. With a hand towel, he patted his face dry, then pulled his fresh T-shirt over his head and tucked it into the waistband of his jeans. He couldn't help comparing the reflection of him in a black T-shirt with Breely in a duplicate shirt. That knot at her hip made him want to untie it and push his hand beneath the hem to touch her naked skin.

If he didn't pull his head out of those kinds of thoughts, he'd have to take the time for that cold shower. After quickly combing his hair, he brushed his teeth and left the bathroom.

He found Breely staring out the window again.

"They call New York City the city that never sleeps." She turned to Moe with a twisted smile. "I think Denver might be the same. Back on the ranch, we were in bed by nine-thirty. It took me a while to get used to working the Friday and Saturday night shifts until 2:00 am."

"Does anyone ever get used to working that late?" He held her jacket up for her to slip her arms inside.

She pulled it over her shoulders and turned with a smile. "I learned to sleep late the next morning."

"You can sleep in tomorrow." Moe folded his leather jacket over his arm, still too hot to wear it. "We don't have to fly out at ten o'clock."

"I'm not on the schedule to work tomorrow at the tavern, but I need to log in and check my emails for the foundation."

"Take all the time you need." He didn't bring up the fact that going back to work at the tavern probably wasn't a good idea. She'd had enough thrown at her for one day. He'd try to make the rest of the evening relaxed and non-confrontational.

He opened and held the door for her.

As she started through, she touched a hand to his chest, sending a bolt of electricity sizzling through him. She tipped her head back, and her green-eyed gaze met his. "I'm not always so hard to get along with. And I don't want you to think I'm ungrateful for all you've done. I do appreciate that you saved my life. It's just…" Her gaze dropped to where her hand lay on his shirt.

"It's just that you're with a man you don't know, and you're hanging onto your newfound independence by a hair." He closed his hand over hers and squeezed gently. The warmth of her small hand in his made him instantly aware of his mistake. Now that he held her hand, he couldn't let go.

He pulled her past the threshold into the hallway. Moe didn't release his grip on her hand. Nor did he hold tight. If she wanted to be free, all she had to do was tug gently.

They walked down the hall, rode the elevator and stepped out on the street hand in hand.

They walked several blocks before Moe's stomach overrode other parts of his anatomy, reminding him he was hungry. At about that time, he found an Irish pub. "Do you like Irish food?" he asked.

"I don't know." Her eyes brightened. "I do like potatoes and lamb."

He opened the door, and they entered. The place was hopping with people crowded around the bar, watching a soccer match on the televisions hanging from the ceiling.

All the tables were full, as well as the seats at the bar.

Moe was about to turn and leave when a couple rose from a booth in the corner. Moe hurried Breely over to claim the table.

A man with a large plastic tub arrived, scooped the dirty dishes into the tub, wiped the table and left. He was followed quickly by a waitress to take their drink orders.

Breely surprised Moe by ordering a Guinness.

"What?" she said with a frown. "I lived on a ranch. We drink beer after a hot day in the sun. My dad prefers Budweiser. Mom and I like Guinness."

"I'll have the same," Moe said.

When the waitress returned with their beers, Moe offered to order for Breely, choosing shepherd's pie. He ordered fish and chips for himself. "If you don't like the shepherd's pie, you can have the fish and chips. I like both. Or we can share."

She grinned. "Sharing sounds good."

When the waitress left with their order, Moe lifted his bottle of Guinness. "To new friends and new experiences."

"To both." She tapped her bottle to his and took a long swallow.

A band warmed up in the far corner of the pub. Soon, a fiddle played a lively tune, and one of the band members sang a bawdy song of the love and loss of a red-haired Irish lass.

Moe couldn't stop the grin from spreading across his face. "Fitting, wouldn't you say?" He chuckled as the music died down.

The waitress arrived with a heaping plate of beer-batter fried fish and chips and a huge bowl filled with Shepherd's pie.

Breely dug into the garlic mashed potatoes on top to find beef tips, carrots, leeks and peas soaked in a thick, rich gravy. When she bit into the first bite, she moaned as she chewed and swallowed.

The sexy sound made Moe's groin tighten. Would she make similar noises during an orgasm? Eating food shouldn't be turning him on.

After she'd swallowed her second bite, she moaned again. "Shepherd's pie, where have you been all my life?"

Her orgasmic enjoyment threatened to kill Moe's appetite for food. He focused on the fish and fries, avoiding looking at Breely as she moaned her way through half of her meal.

He breathed a sigh of relief when she set her fork aside and leaned back. "I can't eat another bite."

"You haven't had a taste of this fish yet." He cut a small chunk off and held out his fork.

She groaned as she leaned forward, took the morsel into her mouth and chewed slowly. "So good."

This time when she leaned back in her chair, she took her beer with her and finished the last few swallows.

The waitress appeared. "Would you like another?"

"I have nowhere to put it." Breely patted her flat belly in Moe's black T-shirt, making him wish he was in that shirt with her hand patting him.

The band had taken a break making it possible to hold a conversation without shouting over the music.

Though Moe continued working his way through his fish, he wasn't hungry. His lusty thoughts consumed him, worrying him. How was he supposed to get any sleep in the same room with the fiery redhead who enjoyed her food as much as he enjoyed sex?

Breely's eyes narrowed, and she sat forward. "You know my boring life story. I know next to nothing about you other than you're prior military and work for the Brotherhood."

"Brotherhood Protectors," he corrected. "What do you want to know?"

She tipped her head to one side. "Which branch of service?"

He set his fork down. "Air Force."

Her eyebrows formed a V. "I've read a lot about special forces. However, I don't recall the Air Force having them."

Moe nodded. "We don't, per se. I was a Pararescue specialist or PJ."

"I'm not familiar with PJs."

He downed the last swallow of his beer. "We're highly trained in personnel recovery. We do whatever it takes to rescue American or Allied forces trapped behind enemy lines, surrounded, captured or injured, and bring them home. Quite often, we work alongside other special forces units to achieve our objectives."

She pushed her bowl aside and propped her elbows on the table. "Sounds dangerous."

"It was." He didn't feel the need to elaborate. Many of his missions had been top secret and often bloody and intense.

"Did you learn to fly planes in the military?" she asked.

Moe grinned. "I learned to fly planes on the farm in South Dakota. I had my pilot's license before I got my driver's license and joined the Air Force when I graduated from high school."

"If you like flying so much, why didn't you fly planes for the Air Force?"

His smile faded. "The man who taught me to fly was a member of the Air Force Reserves. He was called to active duty for the war in Iraq. His plane went down in Taliban-controlled territory. They found his plane and his parachute. It took them three days for our Intelligence guys to locate him and another day to send a team in. They were one day too late. The Taliban killed him."

Breely reached across the table and covered his hand with hers. "I'm sorry."

He stared at her small hand on his, the memory of Colin Henderson's homecoming playing in his mind. Of standing with his mother and father at the airport with Captain Henderson's family as the casket was brought off the plane and loaded into a hearse.

Up until that point, Moe had wanted to be a pilot in the Air Force. Seeing the Henderson family standing on the airport tarmac had touched him in a way he hadn't been able to deny. From that moment, he'd wanted to be one of the elite force that went in to rescue fellow soldiers, sailors,

Marines or Air Force personnel from dangerous situations.

"I joined the Air Force to become a Pararescue specialist to bring out people like Captain Henderson. Alive."

Her hand remained on his. "And you did."

He nodded. "I did."

"And now, you're out of the military. You're not old enough to be retired, are you?"

He shook his head. "I left the Air Force after thirteen years."

"Why?" she asked. "Or is it too personal?"

He gave her a tight smile. "I left, hoping to save my marriage."

Breely jerked her hand back and settled it in her lap with the other. "I didn't even think to ask. Are you married?"

He shook his head. "Not anymore. I married my high school sweetheart straight out of school, joined the Air Force and thought we would live happily ever after." He shook his head. "We were dumb kids with no clue how hard it would be away from the only home we'd ever known. I was happy doing what I loved. She enrolled in a local community college. We moved four times in the first two years. She had to drop her classes mid-semester. She eventually signed up for online classes. Money was tight, so she took a part-time job at the base exchange.

"After I completed pararescue training, I was

assigned to a team, which meant another move. I went ahead to my new duty assignment, was immediately deployed, and she was left to manage the move on her own. She had to quit her job and arrange the packing and moving of our possessions to our new location.

"Meanwhile, I was on the other side of the world, charging into danger. I was shot at, had grenades launched in my direction, and nearly died in an IED explosion. I didn't have access to call often. We'd go weeks between communication with our families back home.

"This went on for several years. I'd be home for a couple of months, we'd have to get used to being a couple all over again, and then I'd be deployed.

"When I returned from deployment, I could tell my wife wasn't happy. She'd bounced around from one low-paying job to another, and she'd given up on college. The family we'd always wanted didn't happen, and she was terribly homesick for family back in South Dakota."

"Did she not know what she was getting into?" Breely asked. "I've read enough stories about military families and the hardships they face when their loved ones are gone for long periods of time."

Moe nodded. "I warned her about being gone, but the reality was harder than she'd expected."

"I guess no one really knows what it's like until they've lived it," Breely said.

He nodded. "That was our case. We were young when we married. My training and the missions we performed changed me."

"And you weren't home often enough for her to get to know you all over again."

"Something like that. When I came home from my last deployment, she was gone, along with everything in our quarters except my clothes. She'd arranged to have our household goods moved back to South Dakota."

"Ouch," Breely said.

"She left a note saying that if I wanted our marriage to work, I had to come home to South Dakota for good. Otherwise, I could sign the divorce papers."

Breely covered her mouth with her hand, shaking her head. "The ultimatum."

Moe nodded. "I was due to reenlist that month. She knew it. I chose to get out and follow her back home."

Breely's brow twisted. "But you divorced anyway?"

"I remembered how we were as teenagers—so young, in love and eager for a future together. I thought we could somehow recapture some of that." He shook his head. "I was wrong."

"She find someone else?"

"No. She was home, surrounded by people she

knew and loved, ready to pick up where we'd left off when we graduated high school."

"But you'd changed," Breely whispered.

He nodded. "She was happy to be in that small town, fitting back into her same old life. I tried, but I didn't fit in. The skills I'd learned to become a PJ didn't transfer to civilian jobs. Who needed someone who could parachute into enemy-held territory, fight his way into a hardened compound, and rescue someone who might have been tortured or injured and get them out alive?" He snorted.

Breely gave him a sad smile. "I guess there aren't that many jobs requiring those skills."

"Not in a town of fewer than six thousand people. My wife didn't know what to do with me. I had nightmares where I woke up fighting. She had to sleep in another room. Finally, I pulled out the divorce papers, signed them and told her to have a good life." He looked up into Breely's eyes. "And I left."

"Is that when you joined the Brotherhood Protectors?" Breely asked.

"No. I wanted back in the action but didn't want to go back into the military. So I signed on with Stone Jacobs, another former special forces guy, who'd set up a security firm providing protection for contractors working in Afghanistan. It was lucrative. I didn't have anywhere to spend my money, so I was able to save it all."

"And that's how you were able to afford your airplane. It must have paid really well."

"It did," he said. "But it came at a cost."

Breely propped her chin in her hands. "What do you mean?"

"We were expendable. We were former military—not active duty. The US government was under no obligation to us or the contractors we worked to protect. We were basically mercenaries. Hired guns there to protect non-military personnel. When the US decided to leave Afghanistan, they pulled military personnel and government officials. Anyone else was left to fend for themselves."

Breely's eyes widened. "The Taliban took over even before our military were all out."

"We had to go into hiding. Had the Taliban found us, they would have killed us."

Breely pressed her hands to her cheeks. "How did you get out?"

"The man I was with at the tavern, Hank Patterson, sent a plane and a team to extract us." Moe's lips twisted. "Kind of ironic. The pararescue specialist being rescued. But, if it weren't for Hank and his team of Brotherhood Protectors, I wouldn't be here today."

"And now you work for him." Breely smiled. "Doing what you do best. Helping others."

"That's the idea." Moe motioned for the waitress.

"Now that you know my life history, what do you say we check out a comedy or jazz club?"

Breely nodded. "Yes, please. But I'm paying for dinner."

The waitress brought the check. Breely counted out wads of bills she'd earned in tips until she had enough to pay the bill and leave a nice tip.

Moe didn't try to stop her, even though he figured she'd spent most of her cash. The woman was stubborn to a fault. Still, he wouldn't let her go hungry or sleep on the streets.

They left the Irish pub and made their way down the street to a comedy club. The place was packed to the point no one else was allowed to enter until some came out.

They continued past a jazz club with the same story.

"If it's all the same to you," Breely said. "My feet hurt, and I'm tired. Could we go back to the room?"

"Absolutely," he said. "I was just trying to give you a taste of the city."

"And you have." Breely slipped her hand into his and leaned against his shoulder. "I loved the Irish pub, the food and walking along the city streets. And thank you for letting me get to know you better."

Moe held her hand all the way back to the hotel and didn't let go until they crossed the threshold into the room.

At that point, he thought it best to sever the

connection. He had promised not to touch her unless she asked him nicely.

They hadn't known each other long enough to take anything to the next level. He wouldn't push it. It wasn't his style. Women came to him willingly.

His gaze followed Breely as she made her way to the window.

He found himself wishing they'd known each other longer and that she would ask him to make love to her.

The chances of that happening were slim to none.

No matter how much he tried to reason with himself, the devil in the back of his mind was banking on the long shot.

CHAPTER 6

BREELY TOED OFF HER SHOES, then collected her brush and toiletries kit. "If you don't mind, I'll jump in the shower first. I don't take long, and I promise not to use all the hot water."

"Go for it," he said and stretched out on the bed, folding his arms behind his head. "Wake me up when you're done."

Her heart throbbed at the sight of Moe, his black T-shirt with the black denim jeans, lying against the snowy white duvet cover, a strand of his black hair falling over his forehead.

Breely longed to reach out and brush the strand back and drop a kiss on his lips.

Her breath caught and held.

What was she thinking?

That she was alone in a hotel room with a sexy man who'd vowed to leave her alone.

Unless she asked him to do otherwise.

One of his blue eyes opened. "Are you okay?"

Caught staring, Breely's cheeks flooded with heat. "I'm fine," she said and scurried into the bathroom, closed the door and leaned against it, trying to remember how to breathe.

Not wanting to hog all the time in the bathroom, she pushed away from the door, reached in and turned on the shower, adjusting the water temperature to a little more than lukewarm.

A cool shower should help to tamp the flames threatening to overwhelm her.

She'd hoped that getting to know Moe would help to establish a solid friendship. Lord knew she needed friends. Especially one with the kind of skills he possessed.

Getting to know him had blown past friendship to something grittier. Something that made her blood burn so hot that heat coiled low in her belly.

Breely couldn't remember being this attracted to the cowboy whom she now had difficulty recalling his name.

She untied the knot in the T-shirt's hem and slipped it over her head, hanging it on the hook on the back of the door. Her bra followed, joining the T-shirt on the hook. After unbuttoning her jean skirt, she dropped it to the floor and kicked it aside.

She stepped into the shower, still wearing her panties, the only pair she had in her possession.

Filling her hand with shampoo from a dispenser on the wall, she rubbed the soap into her hair, building up a good lather. The soap bubbles dripped off her hair onto her shoulders and over her breasts.

What would it feel like to shower with a man? In particular, the one lying on the bed in the other room? Hadn't they toasted to new experiences? That would be new to Breely.

Her nipples hardened into tight little nubs, soap and water dripping off the tips. She reached up and pinched them, imagining Moe's strong hands in place of her own.

A moan escaped her lips before she could stop it. She tweaked her nipples and massaged her breasts with her palms, loving how it felt, knowing it would feel so much better with Moe's hands. Hands that had held hers as they'd walked along the streets of downtown Denver.

She let her hands drift lower, passing her ribs, skimming over her belly button and coming to a halt at the apex of her thighs. Did she dare pleasure herself? She'd managed to bring herself to orgasms before, which took time and patience. If she did commit, her promise to be quick in the bathroom would be at risk.

Her lady parts clenched and released, a silent plea to go there.

First things first.

She drew in a deep breath, the motion raising her

breasts to the spray. As she released the breath, she slid her panties down her thighs and past her ankles. Holding them up to the spray, she rubbed shampoo into the fabric and scrubbed them clean, rinsed and draped them over the curtain rod.

Hopefully, they'd dry by morning. In the meantime, she had only a few minutes to play.

Breely slid her hands over her breasts and down to her sex, sliding her fingers between her folds. When she touched her clit, she sucked in a sharp breath, electrical shocks rippling through her.

Wow. She was on fire. The slightest touch stoked the flames higher.

With the tip of her finger, she flicked the nubbin ever so softly.

More sensations followed the first. Her channel tightened with a delicious ache she couldn't satisfy on her own. But hell, she was willing to try.

Flicking her clit turned to swirling motions, her finger moving faster and faster.

She turned her back to the shower spray and propped her leg on the tile bench, opening herself to more exploration. While one hand worked the nubbin, she slid two fingers on the other hand into her slick channel.

Faster and faster, she stroked herself. Tension built, and her muscles tightened until that tingling sensation exploded at her center and spread throughout her body.

Her hips rocked with the force of her release as she milked the orgasm to the very last spasm.

She wasn't sure, but she might have moaned a few times. Yes, she'd managed to coax her own pleasurable release, but her body demanded more. Her channel throbbed, unfulfilled, empty and wanting.

Breely turned the water colder until she shivered and shut it off. Her skin was chilled, though she'd never been hotter inside.

The one thing that would satisfy her needs lay on the other side of the wall. All she had to do was ask him to make love to her.

He could say no.

Hadn't he said she wasn't his type?

Breely toweled dry, brushed the tangles from her wet hair and stood at the door. Should she step out naked and ask Moe to make love to her, or pull on his T-shirt, crawl into the little chair and try to sleep?

The cool air made her shiver. Breely lost her nerve and pulled the shirt over her head. She cast a glance at the damp panties and shook her head. Commando, it was!

Taking a deep breath, she stepped out of the bathroom and crossed to the bed. When she wanted to ask him to make love to her, different words came out of her mouth. "Your turn."

"Thanks." Moe rose from the bed, grabbed his shaving kit and entered the bathroom.

Breely grabbed a pillow and a blanket from the

closet and dropped them on the small chair in the corner. Her back hurt just looking at the seat that had only enough room to sit, not stretch out or drape her legs over the arms.

Still, she wasn't going to deprive Moe of the bed he'd paid for. The man had to fly the next day and needed a good night's sleep.

With every movement, the T-shirt fabric brushed against her bare bottom, reminding her she was damned close to being naked. All Moe had to do was raise the hem. Nothing stood in the way should he decide to take her up on an offer.

If she made the offer and asked him to make love to her.

How embarrassing would it be if he declined to participate?

Worth every second of angst if he agreed. She could survive the rejection. What she couldn't live with was regret for not even putting herself out there. She'd escaped home and come this far.

Why stop now?

Because she was a chicken with zero skills in seduction and even less in the art of making sex interesting. What if they did it, and he was bored or repulsed at her lack of experience?

Again. She'd rather live with the humiliation than with a lifetime of regret.

"No guts, no glory," she said aloud.

"Did you say something?"

Breely jumped at the sound of Moe's voice immediately behind her. She'd been so caught up in her internal struggle she hadn't heard the shower shut off or the door open. Spinning to face him, her cheeks burned.

He wore a pair of gym shorts. Nothing else. His bare chest had a light coat of black curls. Six-pack abs led to a narrow waist, slim hips and thick thighs below the shorts.

"You were fast," she said, her voice breathy. She couldn't seem to get enough air into her lungs. Not with him and his naked chest standing so close and... Hell. So close.

He nodded toward the chair. "You can't sleep in that chair."

"Sure, I can," she insisted when she should've asked him to make love to her.

Moe shook his head. "No. You can't. You're small, but even a child couldn't sleep on that."

"I could sleep in the tub." She marched to the chair, collected the pillow and blanket and headed for the bathroom.

"It's wet and hard," he said. "No."

"The floor?" Breely looked up into his face. The words to ask him to make love to her stuck to the tip of her tongue.

"No chair. No tub. No floor." He tilted his head toward the bed. "It's a king-sized bed. Plenty big enough for two people to sleep on without touching each other." He took the pillow and blanket from her hands. "We can even put pillows between us if it makes you feel better."

That wouldn't make her feel better. Inside, Breely was begging Moe to make love to her. However, nothing came out of her mouth. She stood frozen to the floor, her body burning.

Just ask him!

"Moe—"

"Breely—"

They spoke at the same time.

Breely laughed, the sound verging on hysteria.

"Go ahead," Moe said.

Breely shook her head. "No, you go first."

"We need sleep. Neither one of us has to be uncomfortable. Seriously, this doesn't have to be awkward. I'm not planning on making love to you or taking advantage of you in any way. I made a promise, and I won't go back on it."

If she wanted it, damn it, she had to take the bull by the horns and own it.

"What if I want you to make love to me?" she blurted out.

He stared down at her without touching her. His eyes narrowed. "Is this hypothetical, or are you asking?"

She slid her tongue across her lips. "Asking," she whispered.

He tilted his head toward her as if he couldn't quite hear what she was saying.

"Damn it." Breely stomped her foot and lifted her chin. "Morris Cleveland, will you make love to me?"

Did his eyes flare?

Breely stared up at him, her breath lodged in her lungs, waiting for his response.

For a long moment, he held her gaze, unmoving, unblinking and completely poker-faced.

Breely teetered on the verge of accepting the inevitable, grabbing the blankets and locking herself in the bathroom for a long night of cursing and sexual frustration.

Her muscles bunched for flight.

Moe raised a hand and cupped her cheek. "Are you sure that's what you want? We barely know each other."

"I know your life story; you know mine." she laughed shakily. "What more do we need to know?"

He brushed his thumb across her cheek. "What's your favorite color? Do you have a favorite flower? Are you a dog person or a cat person? Do you have a favorite side of the bed you like to sleep on?" His thumb slid across her bottom lip. "What are your views on foreplay?"

Breely held his gaze with a steady one of her own. She knew what she wanted, and she was going all in to get it. "Blue. Tulips because they remind me of spring. Dog. The right side. Overrated." She laid a hand on his bare chest. "I've asked. It's now your choice."

Her heart beat hard in her chest, her pulse pounding so fast she was afraid her veins would explode with the force of it. The seconds ticked by so slowly she thought she'd die.

When Moe opened his mouth...his lips moved and then closed tight. He bent, gathered Breely in his arms and carried her to the right side of the bed, laying her gently on the sheets. "You're free to stop me at any moment. I can't promise it'll be easy, but I will stop."

She reached up and cupped his cheeks in her palms. "I want you to stop..." she leaned up and touched her lips to his, "stop talking and start making love to me."

He smiled and pressed a hard kiss to her lips. As he lingered, his mouth gentled, and his tongue pushed past her teeth to glide along hers, claiming it in a sensuous dance.

The kiss stole her soul and her breath, leaving her shaking with the feelings it provoked.

Moe straightened beside the bed. "I'll be right back." He returned to the bathroom.

Breely lay on the bed as if her life was a movie on pause. Everything inside was frozen on the screen, ready to resume as soon as the master hit the play button.

A second passed, then another.

Moe emerged from the bathroom and held up an accordion of condoms with a grin.

The play button engaged, and Breely laughed. "Think we'll use that many tonight?"

"A man has to have goals, doesn't he?" Moe tossed the condoms on the pillow beside her, hooked his thumbs in the elastic band of his shorts and shoved them over his hips. The shorts fell to the floor.

Breely's gaze swept his length from head to toe, coming to rest on the jutting evidence of his desire for her.

Her chest swelled, and her channel creamed. She'd made him that hard, and she wasn't even fully naked yet.

Eager to remedy that, she reached for the hem of the T-shirt.

His hand captured hers and lifted it to his lips, pressing a kiss into her palm. "Let me. It's like opening a present."

His voice melted into every pore of her skin.

As soon as Moe released her hand, she wrapped it around the back of his neck and pulled him down for another one of those toe-curling kisses that made her heart falter and the world outside come to a halt.

Again, Moe straightened.

Breely leaned up on one elbow. "Going for more condoms? You really are aiming for your stretch goals."

He chuckled and walked to the other side of the

bed. "One of my goals is to give you multiple orgasms. It's not a stretch. It will happen." He slid his hands across the tops of her feet and ankles, pausing to grip each ankle. He lifted them and placed them far enough apart that he could lie down between them.

Still leaning up on her elbows, Breely's breathing grew more labored.

Moe brushed his fingers across the insides of her calves and up to tickle the backs of her knees. Climbing up the bed, inch by inch, he followed his finger with his tongue and lips, flicking and kissing a path north to his target.

He pushed her knees up and let her legs fall wide, leaving her exposed to the blitzkrieg of his touch.

Breely had never known how sensitive her inner thighs were until Moe blazed a trail along them all the way up to the center of her desire. Every flick and tender kiss sent shivers across her skin, increasing her anticipation to a fevered pitch.

Moe parted her folds with his thumbs and bent to touch his tongue to the very spot she'd teased not long ago in the shower.

Still hypersensitive from her earlier attentions, the nerves in her clit vibrated, sending shocks of sensation throughout her body.

Breely dug her hands into Moe's hair and moaned.

"Like that?" he murmured, his breath hot on her sex.

"Yes," she said, barely able to push air past her vocal cords.

He touched her again, and lightning sparked inside her. When he swirled his tongue around and around the nubbin, she bucked beneath him, her hips rising, urging him to take more.

Moe continued to stroke her there until he teased the right spot enough times that he set off an explosion of energy bursting through Breely's body, lighting up her nerves like roman candles.

She pressed her heels into the mattress and raised her hips. Her belly clenched, and her body pulsed to the rhythm of her release.

Maintaining his swirls in tight circles around her clit, Moe persisted until Breely collapsed to the mattress, aftershocks of the orgasm making her catch her breath.

Then she tightened her hold on his hair and urged him up her body.

He laughed, rising over her, dropping kisses along the way. One to her belly, one to each of her breasts and the pulse thundering at the base of her throat. When he reached her mouth, he claimed it, diving deep to caress her tongue in a long, slow dance that left her breathless and wanting more.

Then he lifted himself off her and knelt between her legs while reaching for the condoms.

"Let me." Breely snagged the strip, tore one off and ripped it open. She rolled the rubber over his engorged cock, loving how long and hard he was.

For her.

And soon, he'd be inside her, filling a void she hadn't been able to do on her own.

Once sheathed, he settled between her legs and pressed his shaft to her dripping entrance, dipping in to coat himself in her juices.

Past patience, Breely gripped his butt cheeks and brought him home, slowly, easing his thickness into her tight channel.

When she would've pulled stronger, he held back. "Easy. Let yourself adjust," he whispered.

"Want you," she moaned. "Now." Her fingers dug into his flesh, bringing him the rest of the way home.

For a long moment, he didn't move, allowing her channel to stretch and accommodate his girth.

She filled her lungs several times and then tightened her grip on his hips, easing him out and then back in again. With each stroke, she increased the speed until he took over, thrusting again and again.

Breely wrapped her legs around his waist, rode him to the edge and shot to the stars, her body radiating the heat of the sun like a solar flare.

Moe's muscles tensed, and his breathing grew more ragged by the second. He thrust again, driving deep and hard, sheathing himself all the way to the hilt. He came in the throes of Breely's second orgasm, his hips rocking gently, milking every last bit of his release.

Breely collapsed against the pillow and closed her eyes.

Moe's body slackened, the tension easing. He dropped down on Breely, his naked chest crushing her breasts. Then he rolled her with him to their sides and held her cradled in his arms.

"Wow," Breely whispered. "Is it always this intense?"

He chuckled. "If you're doing it right and feeling it."

"Oh, I think we were doing it right." She drew in a deep breath and let it out slowly. "And I was feeling everything." Breely yawned. "Are we going to make it through all those condoms?"

He brushed his lips across her forehead. "Maybe not tonight."

"Will there be another time?" she asked, her thoughts and voice fading. She couldn't keep her eyes open.

"It's a distinct possibility." Moe brushed a strand of her hair back from her forehead, his touch gentle.

She covered her yawn. "Do I have to ask again?"

"Always, sweetheart."

"Moe," she said.

"Yes, Breely." He studied her face in the dimming light.

"Will you make love to me?" She smothered another yawn. "Not now. Later today."

He chuckled. "Sleep, sweetheart."

"Will you be here when I wake?"

"Yes," he said. "I promise."

Her eyes opened, and she stared up into his face, a frown denting her brow. "You didn't answer when I asked." Her frown deepened. "Did I not satisfy you enough?"

"Oh, babe…" He pulled her into his embrace and rested his cheek against her temple. "You were amazing and satisfied me, for now."

"Only for now?"

"Babe, I don't think I could ever get enough of you."

"You won't wake up in the morning with regrets?"

"Only one," he said and kissed the tip of her nose. "That the night was too short."

CHAPTER 7

MOE LAY HALF AWAKE, mostly asleep, with Breely's warm, naked body spooned against his. He knew he should get up and get moving, but he liked where he was with the redhead in his arms.

Sunlight peaked around the edges of the blackout curtains he'd drawn the night before. He turned his head toward the clock on the nightstand.

The green display read 9:58 am.

He groaned. Checkout in one hour. Barely enough time to make love once more, clean up and check out of the hotel.

He could call the desk and ask for a later check-out, but that would require moving away from Breely's delicious body and waking her.

She had to be exhausted. They'd fallen asleep around midnight, woke up to make love near two and then again at five. He smiled at what was left of the accordion of condoms. They'd made a dent in the number. But they could do more if he woke her now.

He didn't have the heart when she'd been through so much the day before.

Breely stretched out her leg, draping it over his thigh, her bottom rubbing against his rock-hard cock.

Her hand slid behind her back and captured his shaft. "Again?"

"Not unless you want to. I wake up this way, especially when I'm with a beautiful woman." He caressed her hip.

She rolled over and snuggled against his chest. "What time do we have to check out?" Her voice was husky with sleep and sexy as hell, making his erection even harder, if that was possible.

"Eleven." He pressed kisses to her forehead and eyelids. "Unless I call and ask for a late checkout."

She leaned up, glanced over his shoulder at the clock and dropped back to the pillow. "We have time."

Thirty minutes later, they were still in bed, naked and sated. Breely from her release during foreplay. Both from riding hard and fast, and culminating in simultaneous climaxes.

In Moe's book, it didn't get better than that.

For a woman who wasn't very experienced with making love, Breely caught on quickly and tried things she thought he might like.

"Where did you learn to do that?" he'd asked at one point.

She'd blinked at him with unholy innocence. "I read a lot."

He'd laughed out loud at the comment and her sad attempt at being completely naïve. She might not have participated in gratuitous sex, but she'd *read* enough to know a little about effective methods of stimulation.

"What book?" he'd asked.

"The Kama Sutra, of course."

Now, she rested her head in the crook of his arm, her hand on his chest, which was rising and falling with each of his breaths as if her hand were a part of him, moving to the rhythm of his body,

"We really should get moving," Breely said. "I'd like to go back to my apartment sometime today and salvage whatever I can."

"You want the bathroom first?" he asked.

"No." She gently dug the tips of her fingers into his skin. "I want both of us in the bathroom at the same time." She tossed aside the sheet and swung her legs over the side of the bed. "I've never showered with a man. I've been skinny dipping in a creek but never shared a proper shower with a man."

Moe stood, rounded the end of the bed and scooped her up into his arms. She was light and easy to carry into the bathroom, where he sat her bare bottom on the counter.

She squealed. "Cold!"

He smacked her thigh. "Good. Maybe you will cool off while I get the temperature right." Moe stepped into the shower, turned on the water and adjusted the heat.

When he turned back to Breely, she sat with her legs spread wide, her fingers sliding between her folds. Her gaze met his, sending a wave of super-nova heat flooding throughout her. "I don't want to cool off..." She sucked in a sharp breath as she touched her slit. "Yes. Yes. There it is." She flung back her head and closed her eyes, her hips rocking with her self-induced release.

What Breely was doing to herself brought Moe's flagging staff to immediate attention. Her cheeks had twin spots of color, and her eyelids sank to half-mast, giving her an expression of raw, unbridled lust. Moe curled his hands into tight fists to keep from grabbing Breely and thrusting deep inside her where she sat perched on the counter. He wanted her to have her climax and ride it to the end.

He tried counting to ten to calm his racing pulse, made it to three and stalked toward her.

Her lips curled into a sexy smile. "Took you long enough." She rested her hands on his hips, guiding him in.

He took her in one swift thrust, burying himself deep inside.

Her channel contracted around him, holding him there as he fought to keep from coming.

"Damn," he gritted out between clenched teeth.

"What?"

"Protection." He pulled free, dashed into the bedroom and returned with the last of the strip of condoms.

She took it from him, her breathing ragged, hands shaking as she tore open the packet. With both hands, she rolled it over his thick shaft all the way to the base, fondling his balls as an added bonus. Then her hands were on his hips again.

He was inside her in a second, scooping her off the counter.

Breely wrapped her legs around him as he stepped into the shower, positioning them under the warm spray.

He let the water soak them, rivulets running over their heads, shoulders and backs. Then he turned, pressing her back to the tile wall.

She braced her arms on his shoulders as he pumped in and out of her, increasing the pace and intensity with each thrust until he was on fire inside, the flame rising, jettisoning him over the edge.

The force of his release had him pulsing inside her for several long, delicious moments. As his heartbeat slowed, he lifted her off him and stood her on her feet, holding her in his arms until he could breathe normally again.

"You are amazing," he said, resting his forehead against hers.

"Until you, I thought orgasms were all hype." She laughed. "Boy, was I wrong." Breely squirted soap into her hands, built up a lather and spread it over his chest.

He armed himself with his own suds and treated her to the same. Soon they were covered in bubbles, laughing and playing beneath the now-tepid spray.

Moe was rinsing Breely's hair when loud banging sounded on the door to the room. They'd left the bathroom door open and heard it clearly.

"What the hell?" Moe shut off the water and reached for a towel.

Before he could hand it to Breely and wrap one around himself, the door burst open, and a tall man strode in, his face a mask of anger.

He marched up to Moe, towering over him. "What have you done with my daughter?"

Breely stepped up beside him on the cool tiles of the bathroom floor, wrapping a towel around her naked body. She lifted her chin and glared at the big man. "Daddy, what gives you the right to barge into this hotel room?"

"The US Marshalls, FBI, Denver police and my name on your birth certificate give me the goddamn right to look out for the welfare of my only child. Especially when she has been kidnapped and taken

ELLE JAMES

across state lines." He tipped his head toward Moe. "Arrest this man."

Breely stood toe-to-toe with her father, a clear foot shorter, dripping wet and barefooted. And she was fierce. Her green eyes flashed. Her chin jutted out. Despite her diminutive stature, she was a Valkyrie ready to bring down the wrath of the gods on her father. "On what charges?" she demanded.

"Kidnapping, assault…" Brantt's gaze swept over Breely in her towel and Moe, who'd wrapped a terrycloth swath around his waist, "and rape."

The Denver police officers pushed past Brantt and grabbed Moe's arms.

He stood tall, holding onto his towel and pride. Resistance would only give the officers a reason to hurt him. The truth would come out, he'd be released, and they would all laugh about the misunderstanding over a beer.

The rage on Brantt's face told a different story. An outcome that could be influenced by wealth and status.

Still, Moe didn't fight the police officers. "At least let me put on a pair of pants," he reasoned in a clear, calm tone. No attitude, no sarcasm. No reason to hit him with a stun gun or pin him to the ground. If the situation didn't improve quickly, Moe would ride it out until he could place a call to Stone and Hank. They had connections. Hopefully, their connections had as much pull as Robert Brantt's.

"This is insane." Breely's stepped closer to her father and turned those compelling green eyes up at him, her eyebrows dipping low. "Daddy, Moe didn't kidnap me. He rescued me from kidnappers who attacked me in Bozeman. If you want to arrest someone, find and arrest them before they make another attempt."

"If this man didn't kidnap you, why did he abscond with you and fly you all the way to Denver?" Brantt glared at Moe. "He's either going to hold you for ransom, or he's going to sell you into the sex trade."

"That's not what's happening here," she said, her tone evening out, her lips pressing into a tight line. "I'm going to get dressed." She pointed to the police officers. "You're not going anywhere with that man until we get this straightened out."

Breely marched into the bedroom and grabbed the black T-shirt and Moe's jeans.

She passed the officers holding Moe, tossed the jeans at one of them, and said, "Let him get dressed. It's the decent thing to do. Unless he's considered guilty until proven innocent."

Moe fought the smile threatening to break out across his face.

When riled, Breely was kickass. A petite force to be reckoned with. She stared at the police officers with her narrow-eyed glare. "I mean it. Don't even think of leaving with that man until I'm back." She entered the bathroom and closed the door.

The officer holding Moe's jeans patted down the denim. When he was satisfied no weapons were hiding in the pockets, he slapped the garment into Moe's hand.

The officers released his arms.

Moe dropped the towel, jammed his feet into the legs of the jeans and pulled them up over his hips, tucking in his still-rigid cock. The weight of Robert Brantt's glare bore down on him.

"My contact informed me that my daughter had been kidnapped and taken to the airport in Bozeman."

"Two men jumped me," Breely, her voice muffled, called out from the other side of the bathroom door. "Moe, the guy you're trying to arrest, saved me."

Brantt's glance never strayed from Moe, distrust evident in the snarl on his lip.

Moe couldn't blame the man. He'd received conflicting information, pulled out all the stops to trace them to Denver, and probably flew down in a private jet only to find his daughter with the kidnapper, naked. Yeah, he could understand Brantt's anger and distrust.

If Breely were his daughter, Moe would have jumped to the same conclusions and might have taken matters into his own hands and decked the naked man, presumably raping his daughter.

Moe nodded toward the T-shirt lying in a wad on top of the dresser. "Do you mind?"

The closest officer grabbed the T-shirt, felt it for weapons and flung it at Moe.

Moe pulled it over his head and tucked it into the waistband of his jeans.

Better. At least he wasn't clutching a towel over his dick, stoking the rage in Breely's father.

"I'm still not convinced you weren't in on the attempted kidnapping. You could have staged it all to earn my daughter's trust."

"He's not the bad guy." Breely flung open the door, dressed in the T-shirt and jean skirt with her wet hair neatly brushed straight. "Daddy, this is Morris Cleveland. Moe, to his friends. He's prior military, a war hero."

"War heroes can have mental issues," her father pointed out.

Breely planted her fists on her hips and pressed her lips together in a tight line. "Have your informants or fact checkers look him up. He's a legit good guy."

Moe's lips twitched at Breely's defense of him. She didn't have to. But she was fierce and didn't back down from the formidable Robert Brantt.

Finally, the older Brantt shifted his watchful gaze from Moe to his daughter. "Then why did he fly you to Denver if he didn't have ulterior motives for you?"

"He was in Bozeman, waiting to fly a medical mission to Denver."

Her father crossed his arms over his chest. "Medical mission?"

"Organs harvested from a crash victim in the Bozeman area had to be flown to Denver. The ambulance met us at the airport," Moe explained.

"It's all documented." Breely waved a hand. "Please, have your spies check it out. And next time, don't accuse someone of kidnapping until you get your facts straight."

"So, Mr. Cleveland had a reason to be in Denver. That's no reason for him to take you and set off a manhunt."

"Whomever your informant is, he needs to get his story straight before he sets off the alarms." She stared at her father, her brows forming a V. "I should've known you'd have someone watching me."

"Obviously," her father said, unapologetic. "You still haven't explained why Mr. Cleveland forced you to fly with him to Denver."

"I didn't force her to come with me," Moe said. "I highly suggested she come since I had to leave immediately, and she wasn't safe to stay by herself."

Breely lifted her chin. "My apartment had been broken into. Everything in it was trashed and the tires on my car slashed. I had nowhere else to go. So, I chose to accompany Moe on his mission to ferry organs to transplant patients."

Brantt had nothing to say about Moe's mission.

"Are you satisfied that Moe didn't kidnap me?" Breely asked.

Her father snorted. "His story makes a little sense. I still don't trust him."

Breely turned to the officers who'd witnessed their family squabble. "As you can see, there's no one to arrest. No kidnapping took place, thanks to Mr. Cleveland. You're not needed here after all." She gave them an apologetic smile. "I'm sorry we've wasted your time. Thank you for your service and prompt response."

The Denver police officers started for the door.

"I didn't say they could go," Brantt's deep voice cut the air like a knife.

The two policemen stopped.

"Uh, sir, the young lady said she wasn't kidnapped," one of the men in uniform said. "We can't arrest this man if he hasn't committed a crime."

"How do we know she's not under duress?" Brantt asked. "He could have threatened to kill her or someone she cares about if she tells the truth."

"Daddy," Breely shook her head, "don't continue to make this difficult. These men have real jobs to do other than catering to you and your unfounded claims." She tipped her head toward the door. "Go. There's nothing here for you to see."

The police officers' gazes went to the older Brantt.

Breely's father's mouth pinched. For a moment, Moe thought he'd say something biting. Eventually, he jerked his head toward the exit. "You can go."

The lawmen hurried through the door before Brantt could change his mind.

Out in the hallway stood a man dressed in hotel livery and two hulking men, wearing black suits and dark sunglasses, that Moe guessed were Brantt's bodyguards.

The hotel staff member had to have been the one to let Brantt into the room. Moe would have a chat with the man after the dust settled.

The door closed on the three in the hallway, leaving Brantt, Moe and Breely alone in the room.

"How long have you known this man?" her father asked.

Breely and Moe exchanged a glance.

"I met Moe yesterday," Breely admitted.

"Then why the hell are you in the same hotel room with this man and…and…" Her father waved a hand toward the bathroom.

Breely cocked an eyebrow. "Naked?"

The elder Brantt's cheeks flushed a ruddy red. "You don't know this man. I don't understand."

"Daddy," she said, "I'm not your baby girl anymore. I'm a full-grown adult. I get to choose how, where I live and who I sleep with. Moe doesn't work for you. You can't make him disappear."

"You don't know what I'm capable of," her father said in a low, dangerous tone.

"Stop pretending you're God and that you can call all the shots." She sighed and touched her father's arm. "I know you and Mama want to keep me safe for the rest of my life, but I can't live the way I did. I felt like I was in prison and hadn't actually gotten to live."

Her father covered her hand on his arm. "I knew you weren't happy. That's why I let you leave."

Her lips curled in that sassy way which made Moe want to pull her into his arms and kiss her long and hard. She was beautiful, feisty and petite, the kind of woman a man wanted to protect.

And she hated being smothered and coddled.

She looked up at her father, frowning her disappointment. "You let me leave and yet sent a spy to keep an eye on me?"

He shook his head. "I sent a bodyguard. He was supposed to stay far enough away not to interfere with your independence, yet close enough to help if you got in a bad situation."

"I'm sorry to say not only is your bodyguard feeding you misinformation he was nowhere around when I was attacked." Breely hooked her arm through Moe's elbow. "This man single-handedly fought off the two attackers and rescued me."

Her father pushed a hand through his shock of

white hair. "The attack in Bozeman is a prime example of why you're not safe off the ranch."

"I'm not going back except for the occasional visit. There's a whole wide world out here. I don't want to miss any of it."

Robert Brantt took his daughter's hands in his. "It's not safe for you to go galivanting around the countryside alone. That would be a surefire way of making you the target of every opportunist intent on using you as a bargaining chip to get to me."

"I know," she said. "I'd still rather take my chances. I can't live on the ranch anymore. I have to make my own way in the world, like anyone else."

"But you're not anyone else. You're the daughter of one of the richest men in the world. Short of giving away my entire fortune and living in a modest two-bedroom house in some city suburbs, there's not much I can do other than provide you with a body-guard, twenty-four-seven."

"I don't want your money, Daddy. I need to learn how to live on my own and pay my own way."

"Okay. But you need round-the-clock protection. I have a man with me who can do the job. He's prepared to go where you go."

Before her father finished talking, Breely was shaking her head. "No. I don't want your bodyguard."

"You can't get around without one," her father said.

Moe studied Breely's stubborn face. "Sir," Moe cut in.

"What?" Brantt responded impatiently.

"I work for a company that provides protection. Since you're from Montana, you might have heard about it—Hank Patterson's Brotherhood Protectors?"

Brantt's brow wrinkled. "Yes. I have heard of Hank Patterson and the company he based out of his wife's ranch a few years ago. I've heard nothing but good things about what his team has accomplished. In fact, he was going to be my next call. I'd like him to beef up our security system and see if he can find someone I approve of to protect Breely."

"Breely already has protection," Moe spoke clearly, daring the elder Brantt to push back.

"Oh yeah?" Brantt tipped his head to one side. "Who?"

Moe bit down hard on his tongue to keep from spewing sarcasm at Breely's father. "I will provide the protection she needs. If I require additional assistance, the other members of my team can be called in."

Brantt met and held Moe's gaze. "You really work for Hank Patterson?"

Moe nodded. "I work out of the West Yellowstone branch of the Brotherhood, which would also be a good place to take your daughter. The town is small. People look out for each other. We'd stay at the West

Yellowstone Lodge, surrounded by more members of the team."

"So, you wouldn't go back to Bozeman?" Mr. Brantt asked.

"Only initially to gather what we can salvage of Breely's things."

"Excuse me." Breely stepped forward. "Do I have a say in what happens to me?"

"No," Moe and Brantt spoke as one and laughed.

"Not funny," Breely said. "I have a job in Bozeman. That job gave me the means to be self-reliant. I refuse to be dependent on anyone else ever again."

"I get that. I also get that you're a target and need someone around who has your back." Moe lifted his chin toward the older man. "Your father doesn't want to take away your newfound freedom. He wants to make sure someone else doesn't."

The older Brantt nodded. "You know your mother and I care about you. If you don't let me hire a bodyguard of my choice, choose one for yourself. But make sure he's capable. You mean too much to your family for us to lose you now."

Her eyes narrowed to slits. "If I choose my own *capable* bodyguard, you won't go behind my back and hire another as backup?"

Her father pressed his lips together and waited a full five seconds before nodding. "I won't."

She stared at him a moment longer.

Robert Brantt raised his right hand. "I promise."

Breely gave him a brief nod. "Then I choose Moe and his team of Brotherhood Protectors."

Moe drew in a deep breath and let it out. For a moment there, he thought she might choose to hire someone altogether different than him.

Breely held out her hand to him. "Do we have a deal?"

"Deal." He gripped her hand, surprised at the firmness of her handshake.

Breely turned back to her father, her face softening. "Let Mom know I miss her. I'll be home for a visit soon."

"Please do that." The big man opened his arms.

Breely stepped into them. "I love you, Daddy, but sometimes, you're overbearing."

He stroked her hair. "You give as good as you get, baby. That's my girl."

Breely stepped back, letting his arms drop to his sides. "Now, get home to mom. I bet she's beside herself worrying."

Her father shook his head. "I didn't tell her about your disappearance. She thinks I'm checking on one of my businesses in Denver."

Breely grinned, lighting up the room with her smile. "She's not as gullible as you think she is," she warned.

"I know." Her father leaned down to press a kiss on his daughter's forehead. "I love how smart your mother is."

"She hates when you go to South America, especially when you go to Venezuela," Breely said.

He nodded. "You know how I feel about our work there."

"I know. Hopefully, we're making a difference with the families we're helping." She hugged her father. "Now. You need to go home and let Mom know I'm okay and that I've got a bodyguard looking out for me. We'll be back in Bozeman in a few hours."

Her father gripped her arms and stared down into her eyes. "And then West Yellowstone?"

She grimaced. "I guess. It makes me mad that I have to move when I was just getting settled in."

"You liked being a waitress?" he asked.

She grinned. "Actually, I did. I was with people."

Her father's brow furrowed. "And we're not people at home?"

"You know how I feel. I won't be held prisoner. I need to be out in the real world, not wrapped in a bubble. I'd rather be kidnapped, shot and killed than locked away for the rest of my life."

Moe understood the need to be free.

"Don't wish yourself dead, sweetheart. If freedom is what you need, just be careful. And don't lose sight of those protecting you. If you can't see them, they can't see you." He chucked her beneath the chin. "Don't take too long to come for a visit. Your mother has been so sad since you left."

"Get her a puppy," Breely suggested. "That's what most empty-nesters do."

"We have dogs on the ranch."

Breely shook her head. "Get her a little dog. One that will look like a puppy all its life. A chihuahua, toy poodle or a Yorkie. Mom needs to be needed." She lifted her chin. "I couldn't live at home forever. It was past time for me to move on."

Her father nodded. "I don't like it, but I respect your determination. Just keep me in the loop."

"I will," Breely opened the door. "Now, go. We're supposed to check out...when did you say?" She turned to Moe.

He glanced at his watch. "Five minutes ago."

Mr. Brantt stepped through the door. "In the loop," he reiterated.

"Got it." She closed the door slowly. "Love you."

"Love you too, baby."

Breely closed the door and leaned her forehead against the panel. "That wasn't awkward at all."

Moe stepped up behind her, rested his hands on her shoulders and turned her into his embrace. "You're his little girl. He will never stop worrying about you."

Breely wrapped her arms around Moe's waist. "I know. And I also know I'm not going back to the ranch. I've had a little taste of freedom. I'm not going to backslide into the cocoon."

"Okay, then." Moe kissed her forehead. "Let's get packed up and in the air."

"I wasn't kidding when I told my father I liked being a waitress. I'm going to miss the people and the challenge of keeping up."

Moe brushed his lips across hers. "You'll be around people at the Grand Yellowstone Lodge. Maybe they can use some wait staff there."

Her eyes brightened. "I'd like that."

Moe handed her his cell phone and turned to shove his things into his backpack. "You need to let Stan know you won't be coming back for a while, if at all. Consider this another adventure to add to your story."

Breely snorted. "I worked hard to do things on my own. Yet here I am again, having to rely on others. That was not my intent nor desire."

"Sometimes, life forces you to change directions." He flung the backpack over his shoulder. "Ready?"

She looked around the room and shrugged. "I guess I am."

CHAPTER 8

BREELY LEFT the hotel room with Moe, feeling proud of herself for standing up to her father and sticking up for herself and what she wanted.

Part of her problem was that she was a people pleaser. She didn't like conflict and hated hurting others, which was why she'd stayed with her parents all those years. She knew how much losing her brother to cancer had devastated them—especially her mother.

Her brother had been outgoing, adventurous and loving. Breely had always thought fate was cruel to take a boy before he'd had a chance to live. He'd never been on a date, wouldn't marry and have children and would never know what it was like to hold a grandchild on his lap.

The day her brother had died, Breely hadn't died, but she'd let her grief and the grief her parents suffered hold her hostage. Her life had gone on hold for all those years.

Closing in on thirty, she knew she had to move on. Her parents had to let go.

As they exited the elevator into the lobby, Breely frowned. A crowd of reporters had gathered outside the glass doors, surrounding one person.

Breely cursed and grabbed Moe's arm. "We need to find another way out of the building."

Moe nodded. "Isn't that your father?"

She nodded. "Someone must have recognized him and let the press know he was here."

Moe hurried to the concierge's desk and handed him the ticket the valet had given him the day before. "Could I have my car brought around to a side entrance?"

The man nodded. "Of course." He motioned toward a corridor. "I'll have him bring it to the loading dock at the rear of the building. If you follow that hallway, it'll take you to the back entrance."

"Thank you." Moe took Breely's hand and walked down the hallway to the doorway at the end. He pushed the door open, and they stepped into what appeared to be an office with a glass window over-looking a loading dock.

A woman sat behind a desk, entering data into a computer. She paused long enough to glance up and then dropped her gaze to the page of numbers she'd been working on. "Are you the couple who asked to have your car brought to the loading dock?"

"Yes, ma'am," Moe said.

She touched a button built into her desk, and the lock clicked on the door behind her. Without taking her gaze off the page full of numbers, she tipped her head toward the door. "Stay left of the dock. You'll find a staircase leading down with a door at the bottom. Your car will be waiting for you there."

"Thank you, ma'am." Still holding Breely's hand, Moe led her through the door, skirted the dock and found the stairs.

As the woman had indicated, the rental SUV was parked outside the door. A valet opened the passenger door for Breely and handed the key to Moe.

As they pulled away from the hotel, they swung around the front.

A limousine eased through the throng and stopped at the hotel entrance.

Breely swiveled in her seat as they passed.

The bodyguards had to physically move members of the press to the side to make a path for her father to get to the vehicle.

"How does he do it?" Breely mused. "Everywhere he goes, they're in his face."

"By keeping you at the ranch, maybe he was trying to spare you the hassle."

Breely nodded. "That might have been some of it.

For the past couple of years, he's received a number of death threats."

Moe frowned. "Do they know who's issuing them?"

"Dad has contacts in the FBI and CIA. They say the threats are coming out of Central and South America."

"Does your father have business dealings there?" Moe stopped at a traffic light.

"He has businesses all over the world. And yes, he has holdings in Mexico, Colombia and Venezuela."

Moe glanced her way. "He's received threats, but has anyone attempted to follow through on them?"

Breely nodded. "Six months ago, someone shot at his SUV when he was in Dallas for a shareholders meeting."

"Dallas has its share of random drive-by shootings."

"True," Breely said. "The police found the vehicle the shooter used based on the license plate and description. It had been reported stolen a few hours earlier. Like you, the police called it a random drive-by."

"Were they able to lift prints?" Moe asked.

She shook her head. "It had been wiped clean. Dad gave the police the benefit of the doubt and accepted their explanation."

"But there's more," Moe stated.

"Yes. A month and a half ago, a bullet hit the

windshield of Dad's truck when he was driving into Kalispell. Missed his head by an inch, only because he leaned over to adjust the temperature."

"Damn. Did they find the shooter that time?"

Breely shook her head. "No. The sheriff thought it might be someone hunting too close to the highway."

"Could the sheriff be right?" Moe asked.

"It wasn't hunting season," Breely said.

"Montana's like Texas," Moe pointed out. "Everyone carries a gun. Maybe someone was shooting at a rattlesnake, and the bullet ricocheted off a rock."

"Another coincidence?" Breely shook her head. "The death threats have been escalating over the past year. The day before his truck was hit, he'd gotten a warning. *Stay out of places you don't belong or suffer the consequences.*"

"What's that supposed to mean?" Moe maneuvered through Denver and out the east end, heading for the airport.

"I talked to Dad after the attack near Kalispell. He said there's political unrest in Mexico, Colombia and Venezuela. He relies on local businessmen and politicians to monitor his interests and smooth the way."

"That's hard to do from Montana."

"He's made many trips to those countries and has men living there that he pays to maintain those relationships when he's not there."

"Isn't it risky operating businesses in countries with unstable governments?"

She nodded. "Always. But it's lucrative, and they need what he provides. In return for allowing him to operate in those countries, he's set up aid programs to help the poor. He's even established orphanages to get children off the city streets, fed and educated. His philanthropies help families in rural communities by teaching them better ways to farm, gifting them with livestock or sewing machines, so they have the means to earn money and feed their families."

"You said you work with your father's philanthropic foundation. Is that the same one doing all these good deeds?"

She nodded. "I help by managing the people who provide the training, run the aid and orphanage operations, procure the animals or products and organize the logistics. It's my way of contributing to the family business and building goodwill."

"You'd think these countries would be happy to have your father's businesses there."

Her lips twisted. "You'd think so, but it seems that no good deed goes unpunished. In Mexico, the cartels raided the homes and farms of those people we've helped and stole their livestock and produce."

"There's not a whole lot you can do to keep that from happening. The Mexican government would have to make a big push to rid the country of the cartels."

"I know." She sighed. "In the meantime, all we do is keep trying. Venezuela has been in turmoil for several years. They're going into an election this year. The incumbent, Xavier Salazar, has done more to hurt the country than help. His rival, Jesus DeVita, is running on a campaign to clean up corruption and bring prosperity back to the people. He's received endorsements from more than a dozen countries. Even the rest of the world wants the current president out."

"What are the chances of the opponent winning?" Moe asked as he took the airport exit.

"He has the backing of the people. If he makes it to the election, he could win the popular vote. But based on past experience, anyone who's dared to publicly speak out against the current government has either been thrown in prison or has disappeared."

"Mexico's a hot mess. Venezuela's unstable." Moe drove up to the building they'd passed through the night before and parked in the same spot they'd found the rental. He switched off the engine and faced Breely. "What about Colombia?"

"The Venezuelan government is mad at Colombia, claiming they killed one of their most prominent generals. Rumor had it that this general was terrorizing civilians on both sides of the border. He's ordered raids on villages, killing the men and raping the women."

"Sounds like Colombia did Venezuela a favor."

Moe got out of the SUV and came around to open the door for Breely.

When he held out his hand, she smiled up at him and let him help her out. "Has your father had any dealings with those governments? Has he made someone mad?"

"I don't know. The last time he was in South America, he visited his companies in Colombia and Venezuela. That was over a year ago. He was happy with the people he'd left in charge and touches bases with them often through video conferencing. He was in Mexico City not long ago."

Moe wished he'd known about the shootings before he'd met Breely's father. He'd have taken more time with the man, been more understanding. Brantt was taking the death threats seriously and was worried about his family being caught in the crossfire. The attack on Breely had shaken him enough to fly all the way to Denver to find her.

Moe reached into the vehicle for his backpack and slung it over his shoulder.

Breely slipped her hand in his as they walked into the building.

He liked the way she fit beside him and how she wasn't afraid to take his hand. For a woman who'd led a very sheltered life, she was making up for the lost time by unashamedly seizing the things she wanted. For the moment, it appeared that she wanted him.

His lips turned up on the corners.

He was smiling when he reached the counter, where a different woman from the night before greeted him. She was young and pretty with blond hair and blue eyes.

Moe decided he was more into red hair and green eyes lately.

"May I help you?" the clerk asked.

He gave her his tail number and checked to make sure they'd topped off the fuel tanks. After he paid the bill, he thanked her, took Breely's hand and walked out onto the tarmac.

The sun shone brightly on his plane, glinting off the blue and gold stripes running the length of the fuselage.

Flying never got old to him. He liked the challenge it represented, the freedom from road-raging vehicular traffic and the peacefulness of being surrounded by blue sky, puffy white clouds and nothing else for miles.

A chuckle beside him made him glance down at Breely. "What's so funny?"

"Nothing. Just that you look like you're in heaven and damned proud of it." She lifted her chin toward his plane. "You like flying that much?"

He nodded. "I do."

"I love that you're passionate about it. Not many people know how to fly an airplane. That makes you special."

ELLE JAMES

"Anyone can learn."

"But they don't."

He unlocked the door, tossed his backpack inside and helped Breely aboard.

For the next five minutes, he conducted his pre-flight inspection of the aircraft, checked the fuel levels and cleaned the front windshield. When he was satisfied the craft was undamaged and flight-worthy, he climbed into the pilot's seat and slipped his headset over his ears.

The next few minutes were spent creating and filing his flight plan. When he was ready and ground control gave him permission, he taxied to the end of the runway and took off.

Soon, they were high above the ground, heading north to Montana.

They spent the next few hours getting to know each other better. Moe asked Breely about life on a Montana ranch and how different it was compared to his life on a big commercial farm in South Dakota.

Where Breely had grown up near Kalispell was surrounded by mountains, streams and trees. The farmlands of South Dakota were picturesque in their own way, with rolling fields of golden grain and blue skies as far as you could see.

Breely wanted to know what it was like to be in the military, to go through basic training and how it was to train for the elite pararescue units.

He described the drill instructors, how tough they

were on them and how they made them stronger, harder and taught them how to work as a team. The men he'd served with were family. He kept in touch with many of them, some of whom were still on active duty. Others had left the Air Force to pursue civilian careers and spend more time with their families.

"Do you wish you'd never left active duty?" Breely asked.

"Sometimes," he admitted. "I miss the camaraderie and friendships. Fortunately, the men I worked with in Stone Jacobs' security firm helped fill that gap."

"I know you still work with Stone, but what about the others?"

"All of us signed on as a team to stand up the Yellowstone branch of the Brotherhood Protectors." He grinned. "Hank was glad to bring all of us on board, and we were glad to have jobs that could use our unique set of skills."

"Do they know we're coming?" Breely asked.

"You've been with me nonstop since we got to Denver. I haven't had the time to call them. I'll do it when we get to Bozeman. We'll be there for at least an hour, getting your things from your apartment and stopping by the tavern. I know you called Stan, but he might want to say goodbye in person."

She smiled. "I'd like that."

Their conversation helped pass the time. He liked listening to Breely's voice through the headset and getting to know more about her. She might have been confined to the ranch, but she'd been fully engaged in ranch life, riding horses, mending fences and herding cattle from one pasture to another.

"My mother made sure I knew how to cook and take care of a house, even though we had staff to do those tasks." She grimaced. "Not that I'm bragging. It's just how it was. On cold wintery days, Cookie and I liked baking cookies for the ranch hands or creating fancy meals like they served in Paris, France."

Moe stared across the cockpit at Breely. "For a girl who learned to ride before she learned to walk, I'm surprised you willingly spent any time in a kitchen."

She laughed. "What else is there to do when the temperatures dip into the negatives? Eating French food might be as close as I get to France."

"If you want to go badly enough, I have faith that you'll get there someday." He grinned. "Your time off the ranch seems to have unleashed the badass in you if the way you handled your father was anything to go by."

Her lips quirked. "I don't think I'll ever forget the look on his face when we came out of the bathroom in our birthday suits."

Moe's grin faded. "I'm surprised he didn't shoot me on the spot."

"If he'd brought his shotgun, he might have. Fortunately, no one got hurt."

"Or thrown in jail," he murmured.

"I wouldn't have let that happen," Breely said. "My father can be stubborn and cranky, but he can be led to reason."

"I was fully prepared to spend the night in jail."

Breely cocked an eyebrow. "Just one?"

"Hank has connections, so I'm told. He'd have gotten me out one way or another."

"I'm so sorry my father was hard on you. I'm glad he came around enough that he agreed to let me choose my own bodyguard."

"I'm sure he's already been on the phone with his sources, performing a background check on me." Moe's lips twitched.

"Yeah," Breely agreed.

"Good for him and for you," Moe said. "I'd do the same."

"He might even call Hank Patterson personally to see if you really do work for the Brotherhood Protectors."

"I'm glad I met with Hank at the tavern, so my face and name will be fresh on his mind when your father calls."

The ATC contacted Moe with instructions for landing at the Bozeman Yellowstone International Airport.

Moe focused all his attention on establishing a

flight path into the airport and landing the plane with a seventeen-mile-an-hour crosswind.

After taxiing to the FBO, he was directed where to park by ground personnel and shut down his engine.

"We won't be here long. Let's plan on being back here in an hour—hour and a half tops."

Breely nodded. "I don't have much to grab. The apartment was furnished. All I need are my clothes and personal items."

He helped Breely down from the plane and worked with the clerk in the FBO, arranging for the use of a loaner car for the short time they'd be in Bozeman.

The sooner he got Breely to West Yellowstone, the sooner he could work with his team to provide the best security possible for the redhead. He'd get on a video conference call with Hank and his computer guy, Swede, to see if they could add any pertinent information to the scenario.

The more he knew about Robert Brantt's personal and business life, the better prepared he'd be to handle any threat that might be headed Breely's way.

He really didn't like being back in Bozeman, where the two men might still be at large, looking for another opportunity to capture Breely.

Before he left the building, he called the Bozeman

Police department and asked to speak to the detective in charge of the kidnapping investigation.

A few minutes later, the detective responded. "After Mr. Morgan, the tavern owner, briefed us on what happened, we canvassed the area. Some people reported seeing a white van. We viewed videos from security cameras in the area. Several showed the van passing by. None of the images captured the faces of the driver or his partner. We found the van behind an abandoned house on the outskirts of the city. The license plate had been removed. We traced the VIN to a used car dealership in Butte. They hadn't known it was missing from their lot until we called them about it."

"Were you able to lift any prints?"

"We did, but we couldn't find a match on the Automated Fingerprint Identification System. The perps have yet to be caught performing a crime."

"I have Breely Brantt with me. If you discover anything pertaining to the case, please call me at this number." Moe gave the detective his cell phone number, thanked him and ended the call.

Breely looked up at him. "Nothing?"

"They found the white van on the edge of town. They lifted fingerprints but didn't find a match on the database."

She sighed. "I'd have felt a whole lot better if I knew those two were behind bars."

"Me, too." Moe took her hand. "Let's get this over with and move on."

She gave him a determined smile. "Deal."

As he drove out of the airport, Moe kept watching in all directions. If those guys were serious about kidnapping Breely, they'd make another attempt. Hopefully, not in full daylight.

Then again, having failed their first attempt, they might be more desperate and take bigger risks on their next crack at it.

Moe glanced in the rearview mirror what felt like a hundred times between the airport and Breely's apartment complex. At every traffic light, he stared into the cars that pulled up beside him and behind him. He didn't want to be trapped between vehicles and have Breely yanked out of her seat and stolen away.

They made it to her complex without incident. After a quick search inside, Moe determined the apartment was clear of intruders. He stood guard at the door with the broken lock while Breely picked through the disaster that had been her home for the past couple of months.

Since her suitcase had been ripped apart, she found a box of trash bags in the bottom of the pantry and filled two with the clothes that had escaped damage. She glanced into the bathroom, shook her head and joined Moe at the door.

"Got everything?" he asked.

"Everything worth getting." She looked once more at the living room, pressed her lips together and turned. "Do you think the manager is going to refund my deposit?"

He tipped her chin up. "Is that humor, I hear?"

"Sarcasm is as good as it gets." She gave him a weak smile. "I hate leaving it a mess."

"I'll ask Hank if he can get someone to make it right."

"I'll pay him back as soon as I get another job. God, I hate being in debt." She stepped out into the hall. "For that matter, I'm not sure I can afford to pay for a bodyguard."

"Hank would be the first to tell you not to worry about it." Moe closed the apartment door and took one of the bags from Breely. "They take on cases whether the client can afford to pay or not."

They left the building and carried the bags to the loaner vehicle, stowing them in the back.

Moe held the passenger door open for Breely.

As she slid into the seat, she shook her head. "How can Hank afford to run a business like that?"

"Those who can pay, do. And business is booming from what he's told me." Moe closed her door, rounded the front of the vehicle and slipped into the driver's seat. "Not to mention, Hank's married to Sadie McClain. She's one of his biggest fans. Hank saved her from someone who tried to kill her. She knows what it's like to be targeted and believes in the protection services he and his team provide."

Breely's eyes widened. "Wait. What? Sadie McClain? The movie star?"

Moe grinned. "That's the one. After what Sadie went through, Hank realized others might have a need for what people like him can provide. Highly trained, disciplined combat veterans who have performed some of the most dangerous missions and lived to tell about it." Moe started the engine and pulled out of the parking lot onto the street. "He only brings on board the best of the best." Moe glanced her way. "Tumbleweed Tavern?"

She nodded. "I let Stan know I wouldn't be in this week. I'd rather tell him in person that I won't be coming back and why. He deserves to know the truth after all he's done for me."

Moe drove the short distance to the Tumbleweed Tavern and parked in front of the building.

Though it hadn't even been twenty-four hours since the last time he'd been there, it felt like days had passed.

At this same time yesterday, he'd sat at a table with Hank, talking about the job, the team and his future with the Brotherhood Protectors.

As he helped Breely out of the car, he was amazed at how quickly things had changed. From admiring the red-haired waitress to having spent the best night of his life making love to her...

Everything had happened so fast. Would they wake up and realize none of it was real? That what they felt was because of an adrenaline rush, and they'd eventually go their separate ways?

Maybe. Only time would tell.

Until then, he had a job to do.

Protect Breely Brantt, daughter of one of the richest men in the world.

That thought alone should have had Moe shaking in his boots.

CHAPTER 9

"Bea! About time you got back to work," Stan called out from the kitchen through the order window.

The two waitresses Breely had worked with for the past couple of months hurried over to her and hugged her tightly.

"We heard what happened," one said.

"We're so glad you're all right," the other said. "It's scary to think something like that could happen right here."

Their hugs and concern warmed Breely's heart and made her sad she would be leaving them to handle the tables without her. "Thank you," she said, her eyes misting.

They hugged her again and hurried off to take care of their customers.

Breely pushed through the swinging door into the kitchen where Stan manned the grill, flipping a row of hamburgers and slapping slices of cheese on them to melt.

She waited until he placed the cheeseburgers on buns, arranged lettuce, tomatoes and pickles around them, then scooped French fries from the warmer and added them to the plates. With quiet efficiency, he placed the plates on the window ledge between the kitchen and dining room and yelled, "Order up!"

Then he turned and opened his arms. "Bring it in."

Breely stepped into his embrace and was immediately crushed against his barrel chest.

He squeezed so tightly she could barely breathe and didn't care as tears slipped from her eyes.

Stan had been her boss, mentor and surrogate father for the time she'd managed to live on her own after her great escape from the family ranch.

When he finally let go, he crossed his thick arms over his chest and stared hard into her eyes. "Are you going to be all right?"

She brushed away the tears and nodded. "I'm not coming back," she said, choking on a sob.

He nodded. "I know, Breely. You're not safe here."

She frowned. He'd called her by her real name. "You know?"

"That you're a helluva a waitress, and we're going to miss you around here?" He nodded, a smile playing on the corners of his mouth. "Hell, yeah, I know."

She laughed at the fact he avoided repeating her real name. "How long?"

"Since your father came looking for you the day after I hired you."

Her heart sank. "He did?"

Stan frowned. "Now, don't go getting angry. He did what any father would do. He made sure his little girl was all right."

"And I wanted to make it on my own." She shook her head. "So, this was all a joke between you and him?"

Stan raised a thick brow. "Did standing on your feet for eight to ten hours a day feel like a joke?"

Breely shook her head, the memories of how badly her feet had ached coming back to haunt her. "Did he pay you to hire me?"

"Honey, that was all me. I told you…he showed up the day after I hired you. He wanted to make sure I wasn't some sleazy geezer who'd trap you in the refrigerator and harass you."

Her cheeks burned. "You're kidding. What did you tell him?"

"That I love my wife, and no other woman on earth can hold a candle to her." He grinned. "I also said that she'd use my favorite butcher knife on my balls if I even thought about someone else. I kind of like my balls where they are."

"I can't believe he did that," Breely said. "I can't believe you didn't say anything."

"Why would I?" Stan tipped his head toward the dining room. "I hired a waitress. I don't care if she's a princess or a bag lady as long as she doesn't smell bad and can do the job." Stan leaned toward Breely. "You never smelled bad, and you caught on quickly. That's all I asked. Did I treat you any differently than the other waitresses?"

Breely's lips twisted. "No."

"Damn right, I didn't. I yelled at you just like I yelled at the others. I don't have the time or energy to play favorites. Either you work out, or you're gone." He shrugged. "You worked out. And we'll miss you."

Breely hugged the man again, her eyes misting all over again. "Thank you, Stan. You're a good man."

"Yeah. Whatever." His eyes were suspiciously shiny. "Don't forget where we are. I could always use a backup when someone doesn't show up for her shift."

"I love you, too, Stan." Breely left the kitchen before she broke down and bawled like a baby.

Moe followed her through the dining room and out into the parking lot. He didn't say anything, just held her door for her, waited until she was settled in the passenger seat and then closed it.

He hurried around the car, slid behind the steering wheel and drove to the airport without uttering a word.

It took all the time driving from the tavern until Moe parked the loaner car for Breely to get her emotions in check. Had Moe said anything nice or comforting, she would have lost her hold on her tears. She was sad about leaving her new coworkers and boss, but it was more than that. She was going to start all over again, knowing she wouldn't be fully independent or free of her family's impact on her life.

She was Breely Brantt, daughter of Robert Brantt, one of the richest men in the world. Therefore, she would always be a target. If not from opportunists looking for ransom money, then from paparazzi chasing a story. Her brief life as Bea Smith, the waitress at the Tumbleweed Tavern, had been rewarding, but a lie. Stan had known all along who she was. It had only been a matter of time before others would have discovered her whereabouts and attempted to capitalize on it.

Her only light in the darkness was Moe. Yeah, she'd only known him a day, but they'd shared their life histories and so much more in that short time. She felt she knew him better than some of the people she'd worked with side by side on the ranch.

If what they'd shared ended up being only a fling, she'd remember their time together as beautiful and intense.

Moe acted as if it didn't matter that she was the daughter of a wealthy man, but, if he were around her long enough, he'd eventually want out. No one wanted the hassle of living in a fish bowl, every move you made recorded and broadcast in the news or the trash magazines looking for drama, not truth.

Breely's father had sheltered her from so much. Still, no matter how scary it was outside the tight security on the ranch, she refused to go back. This meant she'd always need a bodyguard and would always have to be on her toes, aware of her surroundings and careful not to put herself in a vulnerable position.

Breely climbed out of the car, reached into the back of the vehicle and grabbed the garbage bags full of everything she owned. She squared her shoulders and marched with Moe to the airplane as if she were marching into her future...or a battle. The two were synonymous.

At least she'd have Moe at her side during the transition from Bea the waitress to Breely the client. She wouldn't be as alone as she'd thought she was when she'd left the ranch.

Moe tossed her bags into the plane, then helped her get in. He remained on the ground to perform a quick pre-flight check. Then he climbed into the cockpit, filed his flight plan and started the engine.

Breely settled her headset over her ears and adjusted the microphone to a position in front of her mouth.

Everything that had occurred over the last twenty-four hours roiled in Breely's mind. Through all the images etched indelibly in her memory, the hours spent lying naked in Moe's arms gave her the most comfort.

Ground control directed Moe to taxi to the end of the runway and finally gave him clearance to take off.

Moe pushed the throttle forward, and the plane gained speed, the hangars lined up along the side of the airfield flashing by in a haze.

Breely felt like the plane, everything blurring around her as she rushed toward her future.

Moe pulled back on the yoke.

The plane left the ground and climbed higher, leveling out high in the sky, Bozeman growing smaller with each passing mile.

A rush of panic threatened to overwhelm her. Breely had the sudden urge to get out of the plane. Now.

But they were already too high. She couldn't get out. Her only options were to die or ride it out.

Her pulse pounded, and her breathing grew ragged. She was trapped in the plane and trapped in her life. There was no escape.

Moe's hand closed over hers. "Hey," he said.

She squeezed his fingers hard, her hand shaking in his. She hoped he wouldn't notice.

He'd called her a badass.

Being a badass implied she had her shit together.

In reality, she was sitting in the copilot seat of an airplane, quietly losing her shit.

"Breely," Moe's voice penetrated her chaotic thoughts.

She grunted in response, unsure she could form a coherent sentence, much less a cohesive thought.

"Look at me," Moe commanded.

She hesitated at first and then turned to face him, her eyes wide.

"You're going to be all right," he said. "Just breathe."

When she didn't respond, he squeezed her hand. "Come on. Breathe with me. Out with the old." He blew out a breath. "In with the new." Moe pulled air into his lungs, his chest expanding. "Now, let it out slowly." He released the breath. "Again."

He repeated the exercise until Breely joined him. Breathing in and then out.

After several minutes of this, the tightness in Breely's chest eased, and her hands stopped shaking.

One more breath in, and she let it out. "Thank you," she said into the mic.

"You're welcome. I think you'll like the lodge and all the people in it. You'll meet the other members of my team, every one of them prior military special forces. Our leader, Stone Jacobs, along with Ben Yates, Carter Manning and Dax Young, are Navy SEALs. Hunter Falcon is Delta Force, and I'm the lone PJ. We'll have more come on board soon. Stone's father, John Jacobs, a prior service Marine, owns the lodge. Cookie's the chef and prior Navy. He runs a tight ship in the kitchen. Tinker, the handyman, is a former Army motor pool mechanic. The man can fix anything. Then there are the ladies. Kyla is Stone's woman, a real badass and former assassin."

"What?" Breely blinked, her heart skipping several beats. "Did you just say assassin?"

"Yeah. Kyla. She gave up her assassin's life to work the computers with Hank's tech guy, Swede. They're always on a video conference trying to get past some firewall or another. Best damned hackers around."

"Assassin?" Breely shook her head. "What are you getting me into?"

"The best protection you'll find. Ben's lady is Chelsea. She's a wolf biologist. Another badass. She's in and out of the lodge all the time. Dax and Carter's women don't come around as often. They live and work in Wyoming. Amanda is a counselor on the Wind River Reservation. Lilianna is the US Congresswoman for the state of Wyoming."

Breely's head spun with all the names. "Am I going to be tested on all this information?"

Moe's face was poker-straight; not a muscle twitched around his mouth. "Of course. We require all our clients to memorize the names of all our protectors." His blank expression cracked, and he chuckled. "You only need to remember me. I mention the others so that you know you won't be alone. Not all the guys on my team live at the lodge, but you might run into them on occasion. Hank had the hay loft in the barn behind the lodge converted into our office, murder room or war room—whatever we want to call it. It's where we meet to go over assignments, to work a case or use the computers."

Listening to Moe talk about the people he worked with had a calming effect, taking Breely's mind off the future she hadn't wanted but was destined to have.

She had to admit she was excited to meet the other members of Moe's team. Like Moe, they were combat veterans with a laundry list of skills they brought to the Brotherhood Protectors. Each man was a war veteran, had been in the thick of the action, had faced life and death situations and more.

When she thought of all they'd been through, her troubles were minor in comparison. She'd classify her issues as poor little rich girl whining. The least she could do was suck it up, be brave and be prepared if her attackers made another attempt to grab her.

Maybe she could ask the lady assassin to show her a few moves she could use to defend herself.

Panic attack averted, Breely sat back and tried to remember the names Moe had shared with her.

They had barely gotten up in the air when Moe began their descent into the airport at West Yellowstone on the border of Montana and Wyoming.

Moe brought the plane down, the wheels practically kissing the runway. Once firmly on the ground, he applied the brakes, taxied to a hangar and parked in front of a huge door.

"Stay right here," he said as he got out and disappeared through a small door on the side of the hangar. Moments later, the huge door folded upward. Moe drove out in a gas-powered cart and parked in front of the aircraft's nose. He hooked a bar to the front wheel, climbed back onto the cart, towed the plane into the hangar and turned it around, facing outward.

Moe unhooked the towing cart and parked it against the side of the building. Then he came back to the plane and helped Breely to the ground. He reached into the plane for his backpack and the two garbage bags, laying them on the ground one at a time.

Breely carried one of her bags while Moe led the way to a truck carrying the other bag and his backpack.

"Is this yours?" she asked.

He nodded. "Yes, ma'am." Moe opened the back door and deposited his bag and backpack on the leather seat. He took the other bag from Breely and added it to the pile.

While he loaded their things, Breely walked around to the passenger seat, climbed in and buckled her seatbelt.

The drive to the lodge took them less than fifteen minutes. West Yellowstone wasn't a large town. Most of the people there were tourists who'd come to visit Yellowstone National Park on the other side of the border in Wyoming.

They entered the town from the north and turned right, driving all the way to the western end of town where a grand old lodge stood as it must have a hundred years ago.

Breely got out of the truck before Moe could come around and open the door for her. She grabbed her bags and met him at the front of the truck. Together, they climbed the porch steps to the front entrance.

A man with black hair graying at the sides stepped through the door, his hand thrust out. "Moe." He gripped Moe's hand and pulled him into a back-pounding bear hug. "Glad you made it back."

"Thanks."

"Your trip to Bozeman and Denver turned out a little more complicated than expected." The man released Moe and advanced on Breely. "Breely Brantt. It's a pleasure to meet you. Let me get those for you." He took the bags from her hands.

She stood on the porch, her hands empty. Not knowing what to do with them, she stuck them in the back pockets of her denim skirt. "You know my name, but who are you?"

The man chuckled. "Sorry. I'm Stone Jacobs. Hank called, and then your father called, letting us know you were on the way. We have a room ready for you if you'd like to get settled in first."

"Yes, please." More than anything, she wanted to change out of the skirt and into jeans and one of her own shirts. Though she liked wearing Moe's over-sized T-shirt, she felt like a little girl playing dress-up in it. She liked wearing it better when they were alone.

Stone turned to Moe. "We put Breely in the room next to yours. Since you're taking this assignment, we figured you'd want to stay close."

"Thanks," Moe said. "I do."

Stone led the way, carrying the two bags.

Moe fell in step beside Breely and reached for her hand.

She held on until they entered a hallway and stopped before a solid wooden door stained dark mahogany.

Stone used a key to unlock the door, then handed the key to Breely. He tipped his head to the door beside the open one. "Moe's in that room. There is a connecting door. You can choose to keep it locked, but if you're in any kind of trouble, he'll have to go around. Either way, the doors will be locked, and it will take longer for him to get in."

Stone entered the room, deposited the bags on the bed and came back out. "Cookie serves dinner promptly at six. I don't know what he's making, but it smells good."

"Cookie never disappoints." Moe's stomach grumbled loudly. He glanced at his watch. "We have thirty minutes until six if you'd like to shower and change."

"I would," Breely said. To Stone, she smiled. "Thank you for everything."

"Our pleasure." Stone clapped a hand on Moe's back. "Moe will take good care of you." He nodded to Moe. "See you at six." He left them standing in the hallway and disappeared around a corner.

Moe glanced down at Breely. "Are you okay?"

She gave him a weak smile. "I will be."

He cupped her face in his palm. "Yes, you will." Then he looked up, entered her room and strode to the connecting door, twisted the lock and pushed through to the room on the other side.

"Like Stone said, it's your choice whether you want to keep the door locked or leave it unlocked." He came back to her and captured her face in his hands. "I'd rather you left it unlocked. It doesn't mean I'll consider it an open invitation to visit whenever I like. That will be your choice. I just want to be able to get to you if someone breaks into your room."

She raised a finger to his lip. "Leave it unlocked."

He kissed her finger. "Okay. I'm going to get a shower and shave. See you in twenty-five minutes?"

She nodded.

Moe passed through the connecting door and closed it behind him, leaving it unlocked.

The possibilities that the unlocked door represented warmed her blood and left her body in a delicious sense of anticipation.

Those possibilities would have to wait. They hadn't had breakfast or lunch, and apparently, Cookie liked people to be prompt.

Breely had wanted to get away from the family ranch and experience life.

Well, she'd gotten what she'd wanted and more.

She'd worked as a waitress with some wonderful people, had been rescued from kidnappers by a sexy PJ, had flown in his private plane to Denver and made mad, crazy love through the night with a stranger.

So what if she didn't know what came next? She could be resilient and open to the next great adventure.

She just hoped she'd live to enjoy it.

CHAPTER 10

Twenty-five minutes later, Moe knocked gently on the connecting door between his room and Breely's.

Her soft, "Come in," made his heart skip beats and his blood burn through his veins headed south.

He pushed the door wide and stepped into her room. She stood in front of a full-length mirror, her back to him. Breely wore a satiny, green sheath dress with narrow straps, balanced over her pale, lightly freckled shoulders. The back scooped low, dangerously close to her buttocks. Green silky satin clung to her curves, hugging her like a second skin from her breasts to her hips where the skirt flared out, falling softly past her knees. On her feet, she wore shiny, silver strappy sandals with delicate heels.

Breely had swept her hair up in a loose, messy bun on top of her head, the thick curls wound several times around the elastic band, strands held in place with a few strategically placed bobby pins.

Facing the mirror, she frowned. With a rhinestone-studded comb in her hand, she held it over several locations on her head, shook her head and finally slid the comb in front of the bun, securing some loose strands and adding a bit of bling to already glorious hair.

She met his gaze in the mirror. "Will this do?"

"If by *do,* you mean it makes me want to rip that dress from your body, skip dinner and feast on you for the rest of the night..." he nodded, "it will do." He reached out to place his hands on her hips and stopped before he touched her. "May I?"

"Mmm," she moaned, her eyelids sinking halfway over her eyes. "Please."

Moe rested his hands lightly at her waist. Unable to resist, he slid his fingers over her hips and behind her to cup her ass in his palms.

The dress was smooth and cool to the touch. No matter how chilly, it couldn't tamp down the rising desire coursing through his veins.

Breely leaned her naked back against his crisp cotton, button-down shirt. "How long does it take to walk from our rooms to the dining hall?"

"Two minutes." Moe checked his watch and grimaced. "We have exactly two minutes to get to the dining room. Stone wasn't kidding about Cookie liking people to show up on time." He held out his arm. "Are you up for a sprint?"

Breely waved a hand toward her feet. "In these shoes?"

"I guess not." Moe shook his head. "Then we'd better get going and step out smartly." He held out his arm.

Breely hooked her arm through his, and they left her room.

Moe set the pace, careful not to push this beautiful woman so fast that she slipped, slid or fell in an inglorious heap. Ahead, he spotted Stone standing in the middle of the rest of his team. Kyla and Chelsea stood to the side, their heads together, laughing about something one or the other had said. All attention turned to Moe and Breely as they entered the dining room.

"I guess everyone turned out to meet the new client," he murmured.

Breely's hand tightened on his arm. He reached over and patted her reassuringly.

He should have known they'd be highly interested in meeting Breely Brantt, daughter of Robert Brantt.

Moe would rather have returned to their rooms and had Breely all to himself. He heard a low rumble from the vicinity of Breely's belly. His stomach echoed the sound. Hunger won out.

"We should've eaten lunch at the Tumbleweed

Tavern," he said beneath his breath for only Breely to hear.

"Agreed," she responded without losing the smile on her lips.

They joined the others standing near the long table reserved for them. Other guests sat at tables scattered around the large dining room. Some glanced up to see who'd entered and went back to eating the meal Cookie had prepared.

"Gang's all here," Stone sang out. "Everyone, you know our token PJ, Moe. The lovely young lady on his right is Breely Brantt. She's chosen Brotherhood Protectors to provide the security and protection she needs until we or the authorities locate the men responsible for her near-kidnapping in Bozeman." He waved a hand toward Breely. "Please say hello to Ms. Brantt."

As one, they said, "Hello, Ms. Brantt.

Breely's cheeks flushed a soft pink. "Thank you. But, please, call me Breely."

"Noted," Stone said. "You know Moe. Let me introduce the other members of the Brotherhood Protectors Yellowstone team." He nodded toward a man who stood taller than the rest with an auburn-haired woman beside him. "This super tall drink of whiskey is Benjamin 'Bubba'—"

"Yates," Breely finished. She held out her hand.

He engulfed her smaller one and gave it a firm but gentle shake. "Nice to meet you, Ms. Br—eely." His cheeks turned a ruddy red. He turned to the woman beside him. "This is my fiancée, Chelsea."

The pretty, auburn-haired woman shook Breely's hand with both of hers. She stood at least half a foot taller than Breely, but her smile wasn't the least intimidating, "Glad to meet you," she said.

"Thank you. Are you the one who's a wolf biologist?' Breely hoped she'd remembered what Moe had told her.

Chelsea grinned. "I am. I work the packs in and around Yellowstone National Park."

"How interesting. I understand the reintroduction of wolfs to the ecosystem has helped to create a better balance for the plants and wildlife in the area."

"We're working through issues with local ranchers. The wolves don't care if their meal is deer or beef. The ranchers do, and they tend to shoot the wolves." Chelsea sighed. "It's all a delicate balance. Speaking of which…it's nice to have another female around this testosterone fest. Right, Kyla?"

The same height as Chelsea, Kyla's lean, athletic body looked like she could take a full-grown man down with her hands. Yeah, she was tall and intimidating.

She took Breely's hand in a very firm, almost painful, grip. "Breely," she said with a curt nod.

"Kyla."

"We like Moe," the dark-haired woman stated, her eyes narrowing. "Don't fuck with his head."

The implied *or else* made Breely's knees wobble. "You're the assassin turned tech support." Breely tightened her grip to equal the pressure Kyla was using.

"Don't let Kyla scare you," Chelsea said. "She's retired from her work as an assassin. Now that she and Stone are a thing, she's getting all soft and squishy."

Kyla glared at Chelsea. "I'm not soft and squishy."

Stone coughed, "Bullshit."

"Look. I don't go out and kill people with guns or knives. I know how to inflict more pain and never fire a bullet or wield a blade."

"How do you manage that?" Breely asked. "Are your hands and feet registered as lethal weapons?"

"I guess they could be. But it's not hands and feet I use to cut down my enemies." She wiggled her fingertips and grinned, softening her features to an almost a squishy appearance. "I use my fingers."

"Poke out a person's eyeballs? Sever the jugular. Rip out a heart?"

Kyla's brow twisted. She glanced over her shoulder at Stone. "She's a bloodthirsty debutante."

Breely's eyes narrowed. "I'm not a debutante. That would infer I've been presented to wealthy social circles, attended a posh private school or gone to a cotillion. I've done none of that." She crossed her arms over her chest. "Now, if you need a fence mended, a bull calf castrated or someone with small arms to shoe them into a heifer's hoo-hah to turn a breach calf…" she jammed a thumb toward her chest, "I'm your girl. I can't dance, I'm socially awkward and I've never mastered smoky eyes. I bought this dress online five years ago and never had a place to wear it until now. And these gorgeous shoes are giving me a blister."

"Tell it, sister!" Chelsea gave her a high-five and a fist bump.

Kyla's eyebrows rose into the hair falling over her forehead. "Damn, girl. Remind me not to piss you off. You've got wicked skills hiding under that slinky dress."

"You know you don't have to dress formally here," Stone said. "All Cookie asks is that your jeans don't have huge holes and you wear a shirt and shoes to the table."

Breely laughed. "I should be able to follow those rules with my eyes closed."

Bubba pointed to a red scar on his forehead. "I don't recommend it. This place is a maze. With the lights out, it's exponentially dark and dangerous. Especially for those of us who are vertically challenged by six-foot-tall doorframes."

A man with brown hair and brown eyes elbowed his way past Bubba and held out his hand. "Carter Manning." When she started to take his hand, he pulled back, and his eyes narrowed. "You did wash your hands after sticking it inside that heifer's hoo-hah, didn't you?" He winked and shook her hand. "Nice to meet you."

Another man with brown hair and piercing brown eyes stepped up. "Hunter Falcon."

"You're the Delta Force guy, right?" She shook his hand and looked around at the men. "Thank you for your service to our country."

They nodded as one, all staring at her, expecting her to say something. These men had so much life experience, what could she add that would begin to sound interesting?

Not a damn thing. Silence stretched as Breely scrambled for something intelligent to say, her cheeks heating.

"Take your seats," a booming voice called out, breaking the silence. "Dinner is served."

Moe leaned close to Breely. "That would be Cookie."

A short, stocky man with a shock of unruly white hair and bright blue eyes entered the dining room.

"That's right. Make it quick before this food gets cold." Behind him came an even shorter, wiry man with brown hair and brown eyes. "The second guy is Tinker, our master mechanic."

Each man wore a white apron and carried a platter.

Cookie carried a large platter with a giant ham in the middle and garlic-roasted potatoes all around the base.

Tinker's platter was filled with a medley of vegetables—broccoli, carrots, cauliflower and squash.

The men set the platters in the middle of the table and hurried back to the kitchen, returning quickly with baskets of dinner rolls, pitchers of tea and lemonade.

Everyone settled in seats around the dining table. Chelsea urged Breely to take the one beside her. Moe claimed the seat on Breely's other side.

Platters were passed, food dished out onto plates and glasses filled. When everyone had what they wanted, Breely spent the next few minutes taking the edge off her hunger with the best ham and roasted potatoes she'd ever eaten. Seasoned to perfection, the ham melted in her mouth.

"This so good, Cookie," she said. "Where did you learn to cook like this?"

"Aboard a Navy ship and then at the White House," he responded.

Breely glanced around at the people gathered for the meal. "Is anyone at this table an ordinary person? I feel like an underachiever."

"You're anything but. I don't know many women who can work a ranch, much less have done it for years," Stone said. "You didn't say anything about the work you do for the Brantt Philanthropy Foundation."

"That's right," Kyla said. "I got online and did some research. Your work with the foundation has helped so many people. You've shown hungry families with little to their names how to grow food and raise livestock as well as trained them in specific trades they can earn a living with."

"You should be proud of what you do," Stone said. "Your work in Venezuela has opened eyes and spawned a movement they'll have a hard time repressing."

"Their current president has control of the military," Breely reminded them. "He can and has ordered the police and the military to arrest people who speak out against the current regime."

Stone nodded. "We spoke with your father about the death threats he's been getting. They appear to have started around the same time as the election campaign got ugly."

Bubba nodded. "Brantt said that the last time he was in the country, he met with the opposing candidate, Jesus DeVita. The media captured a photo of Brantt shaking hands with him. It's been all over the news and tabloids. The poor people the foundation has helped are spreading the word that Brantt is backing DeVita and government reform.

"DeVita is showing a strong lead in the polls," Kyla said. "If he wins, the cartels playing Salazar like a puppet will be out. Or they'll have to take out DeVita. It would be easier if Salazar's opponent were eliminated or debunked before the election takes place."

"What if the death threats and the attempted

kidnapping have nothing to do with what's happening in Central or South America?" Breely asked.

Stone's brow dipped low. "Then we need to know about everyone who could have a grudge against you or your father. Anyone who has looked at you cross-eyed."

"It could be anyone," Breely said. "My father is a very wealthy man. Anyone who kidnaps me could ask for a lot of money for ransom. The motivation doesn't have to be personal. Money is a very tempting motivation."

"True," Stone said. "But let's eliminate grudges and payback before we throw the net out further."

Breely nodded. "Okay."

"After dinner, I'd like us to go over to our headquarters in the barn and get on a video conference with Swede and Hank." Kyla laid her fork on her plate.

"You're not finished, are you?" Stone asked.

Kyla stared at the plate of food she'd left untouched. "I'm not hungry," she said. "I want to get started collecting data and digging into the people around Robert and Breely Brantt."

Breely had eaten enough to satisfy her hunger. "I'm ready. The sooner I give your computer guys all the information you could possibly need, I'm going to soak in that clawfoot tub until my skin shrivels."

"That sounds...nice," Chelsea said. "All except the

skin shriveling part." She laid her fork on her plate. "I'm done. The three of us can wander over to the loft and get started with Swede. You guys can catch up when you're done eating."

"I'm going with you." Moe tossed another dinner roll on the plate, covered it with a napkin and pushed to his feet.

The ladies were a little slower making their way to the war room, first carrying their plates to the kitchen and loading them into the dishwasher.

Moe leaned against a counter and continued to eat, one eye on Breely at all times.

Finally, Kyla led the way through the lodge and out a back door. A path of paving stones led to the barn at the back of the property.

Kyla entered and went to a brand-new set of stairs leading up to the loft.

The barn downstairs looked and smelled like a barn should, earthy and filled with the scent of hay and horse dung.

Upstairs was nothing like Breely expected. The loft had been completely remodeled to include drywall, paint, plumbing and electricity. A massive conference table stood in the middle, surrounded by rolling office chairs. An array of monitors filled the wall in the back corner with keyboards ready for use. Kyla went straight to the computer monitors and sat down at a keyboard. Before long, she had the keyboard humming with the speed of her strokes.

Moe nodded toward a door. "That's the armory. Hank outfitted it with everything we could need for any mission, from bodyguard and protection details to small-scale war conducted by members of our team."

Breely's eyes widened. "Why would they do that?"

His mouth pressed into a thin line. "Like when we had a faceoff with a drug cartel running drugs through the Wind River Reservation, which was killing off teens and making it look like suicide when they wanted out. The cartel came to claim their territory. We disabused them of their claim. Hopefully, they won't be back anytime soon."

"Wow," Breely shook her head. "Who even thinks we have wars going on here in the US?"

"You won't see much about it in the newspapers," Moe said. "It happened on a reservation."

Stone, Hunter, Carter, Dax and Bubba entered the war room.

From the corner, Kyla called out, "I've got Swede and Hank on video. Transferring to the big screen now."

The screen at one end of the conference table blinked to life. A giant head appeared before them.

"Have a seat," Stone instructed.

Everyone gathered around the table.

Stone turned to Breely. "Swede, this is Breely Brantt, Robert Brantt's daughter and only living child."

Swede dipped his head. "Breely."

Breely gave a tiny nod. "Swede."

"We spent time at the dinner table discussing political issues that could have put Robert Brantt in the crosshairs of a corrupt government with connections to a powerful drug cartel." Stone gave Swede a recap of what they'd learned from their research based on what Brantt had told them.

Hank's face appeared beside Swede's. "Hey, team. Breely, Chelsea. Glad to see Moe and Breely made it there safely. I hope the flights were smooth."

"Couldn't have asked for better flying weather," Moe reported.

"Good." Hank gave them all a quick smile. "We had a video conference with Brantt as well and went over every employee who worked at the ranch, those who still work there and those who were let go." He nodded to Swede. "Can you put it on the screen for them?"

Swede looked down. The sound of clicking keys filled the silence. Moments later, Hank and Swede's faces disappeared, and a list of names appeared.

Breely leaned forward, studying the list of names she found familiar and some she didn't. Beside the names were listed two dates: date of hire and date of release.

Those without a release date still worked at the ranch. Breely skimmed over their names, familiar with all of them, a wave of homesickness washing over her. She'd grown up around these people, worked alongside them and knew their families, their dreams and sorrows.

None of the full-time employees jumped out as people who would attempt a kidnapping.

She focused on the names of those with a release date. Half of them had left of their own accord.

"Brandt put a star by the names of people who were fired or laid off," Hank said. "It narrows down the list to ten people. We're conducting background checks on those."

"What were the reasons for releasing them?" Moe asked.

Breely knew all of them, going back to when she was a teen.

"Beau Joyner, Randy Denton and CJ Veatch were teenagers Daddy hired one summer, hoping to grow them into ranch hands. They liked to party at night and never made it to work on time the next morning. Daddy gave them multiple opportunities to make it work. He finally had the foreman send them home. It's been a long time. I doubt the few weeks they worked at the ranch made a lasting impression on them."

"We'll do a cursory look at where they are now and dig deeper if there are any red flags," Swede said.

"Cody West." Breely's cheeks heated. She hated how personal this could get, with so many standing around potentially judging her.

"Breely," Hank said softly, "do you want to clear the room except for you, me and Swede?"

She considered it. No one liked airing their sex lives in front of an audience. No matter how well-meaning that audience was.

"Look, if this helps us find who is targeting me and my family, I can stand a little humiliation." She lifted her chin toward the list. "I was sixteen; he was nineteen and an accomplished horseman, a cowboy familiar with wrangling cattle and horses. He had a bright future as a cowboy." She shrugged. "I thought I was in love with Cody West. We steamed the hayloft that summer. Then one day, he didn't show up for work. He never came back." She met Hank's gaze on the monitor. "I think my father paid him to leave."

Hank nodded. "He did. We're looking at him."

"It's been over a decade. Why would he come back to haunt me now?" Breely shook her head. "He's probably married with half a dozen children."

"What better reason to need money?" Kyla said.

Cody hadn't been a bad guy. She'd been young and impressionable. He'd been young and sowing his wild oats.

She moved down the list.

"Steven Ford was caught stealing money and credit cards from other employees. Daddy had the sheriff arrest him and escort him off the property. He was mad. He took a swing at the sheriff's deputy. He blamed everything on my father. Hell, that's been more than eight years. What's the statute of limitations on being pissed for being ratted out to the sheriff?"

"Some people never let go of a grudge," Kyla said.

"Marty Riggs and Taylor Brown were lazy. They didn't last a month. They didn't seem surprised when they were escorted off the property."

"What about Jarod Jones?" Swede asked.

"Too interested in his cell phone and his girl-friend. If you don't focus on the task at hand, you can get hurt or injure someone else. He also liked to say, *That's not my job. I didn't hire on to muck stalls or clean out feed troughs.* When we hire hands, we specifically say they must be willing to do anything. We never know what's going to blow up in our faces, run us down, or break and need fixing."

Hank chuckled. "Sounds like a typical day on the ranch."

"You get it." Breely smiled at the head of the Brotherhood Protectors. She'd heard he'd been raised on a ranch like her. "Dillon Sarley." Her eyes narrowed. "I caught him stealing money from the petty cash in my father's office in the house. Ranch hands weren't allowed into the house without permission. Daddy wanted to call the sheriff, but Dillon begged him not to. He returned the money and promised not to steal from my family again.

"Daddy was in a hurry to get to the airport. He let

Dillon off with a warning to never step on Brantt property again."

"Has he?" Moe asked.

Breely shook her head, "Not that I'm aware of. It's been three years."

"Have you seen him around the town where you live?"

She shook her head. "I heard he had to move away. Since Daddy wouldn't give him a recommendation, no one would hire him. He should've gone to jail. There was over two thousand dollars in that petty cash drawer. He thanked Daddy for not charging him for breaking and entering and robbery. As he left the house, he saw me standing in the doorway to the living room."

"Did he say anything to you?" Hank asked.

Breely closed her eyes and thought back. "He muttered something about me being immature and snitching." She looked up. "He stole almost two thousand dollars, and he was mad at me?" She shook her head. Sometimes, I don't understand people."

"I have difficulty understanding people as well. Was there anyone else on the ranch or in the nearest town who might have held a grudge against your family?" Hank asked.

Breely shook her head. "Not that I can remember."

"Thank you," Hank said. "I know it can be hard to

talk about the past. If you think of anything else, don't hesitate to shoot it our way."

"Will do," she said.

"We'll work these names and get back to you," Swede said.

"I'll work them from here, as well," Kyla said.

"Moe?" Hank said.

Moe straightened "Yes, sir."

"I know we have the right guy on the job. Stay safe and keep Ms. Brantt safe."

"Yes, sir." Moe's hand rested in the middle of Breely's back. He glanced down at her. "Wanna go for a walk?"

She nodded. "I'd love some fresh air."

"Are you done with us?" Moe asked everyone in the room.

"For the moment," Stone replied. "If we need you, we'll find you."

Moe led the way out of the loft and down the stairs. "Woods or street?"

"I'd like to see a little bit of West Yellowstone before dark."

Moe glanced at the sun slowly sinking into the mountain peaks. "Streets, it is. Stay close to me. If bullets fly, I want you on the ground first. We'll figure out how to get away after that."

"Way to take the fun out of a walk," she grumbled.

He grinned. "I'd rather have you aware and alive, than have you die in ignorant bliss."

"There you go, spreading more happiness." Breely stopped in the barnyard "Keep it up, and I'll go for that walk on my own." She stretched her arms over her head, trying to work the kinks of stress out of her shoulders, but that wasn't happening until they found the people responsible for the attempted kidnapping.

She hoped they found the guys before they found her again. In the meantime, she would be jumpy when she thought a shadow had moved. Her heart would race when she imagined seeing someone darting through the woods behind the lodge.

Thankfully, she had Moe looking out for her. She liked that. A lot. Too bad she was just an assignment to him. What would happen when they found the guys? The risk would be eliminated. She might not need a bodyguard anymore. Moe would move on to his next assignment.

Her heart hurt at the thought of losing him. So, she'd stop thinking about losing him and live in the moment.

CHAPTER 11

MOE WALKED with Breely along the touristy streets of West Yellowstone, ducking into souvenir shops, stopping to get ice cream at a specialty ice cream shop and pretending they were just another couple on vacation.

But they weren't.

Moe kept a constant vigilance from all angles around them. He was relieved when she decided they should head back to the lodge.

The lodge didn't boast tight security, but there were a number of his counterparts still staying there. If he needed help, all he had to do was shout, and someone would come running.

Though it wasn't very late, Breely was tired from all the drama and stress of the past thirty hours.

They wandered through the kitchen to fill a

couple of glasses with water and carried them to their rooms.

Moe entered through her door, quickly inspected the space and declared it clear. When he started to go into his room, she snagged his arm. "Where are you going?" she asked.

"To my room," he said.

She stared up into his eyes. "Do you want to go to your room?"

He shook his head. "But I don't presume to know what you want."

"I want you." She smiled and tugged the hem of his T-shirt out of the waistband of his jeans. "Please. Stay with me."

And he did.

That night.

All the next day.

And the next.

A WEEK WENT BY, and nothing happened. No attacks, no death threats. Nothing.

Moe found it difficult to maintain his vigilance. But he did. Since no one had tried to nab Breely, they ventured out, visiting local parks. Moe bought Breely a fishing pole and took her fishing in the nearby river. They cleaned the fish they caught and brought them back to Cookie to prepare in his kitchen.

When she needed hard physical exercise, Breely

mucked the stalls in the barn and lunged the few horses that lived on the property.

On some evenings, Breely worked waiting tables in the bar. She liked being busy.

Moe would help by bussing tables, just to be close to her.

Though they enjoyed their outings, Breely seemed bored. She'd worked on a ranch her entire life. Hard work was what she did. The tavern had kept her moving, never lacking something to do.

Once or twice during the day, she'd log onto her laptop and conduct a meeting with the people working different areas of the Brantt Philanthropic Foundation. She dressed nicely and applied the makeup she'd purchased at a store in town before entering a Zoom meeting.

Moe stayed close by, admiring how beautiful she was. At the rate they were going and the amount of time they spent in each other's company, he was doomed. When he'd divorced, he'd vowed to never marry again.

Yet, here he was daydreaming about what it would be like when they were older, grayer and sitting on a front porch swing with their grandchildren playing at their feet.

He spent every night with her in his arms. He woke with Breely's naked body spooned into his.

He could get used to that. Hell, he already was. Moe never wanted it to end.

They were drinking lemonade on the back porch of the lodge, letting their food digest after one of Cookie's amazing meals.

Stone came out on the porch. "Got a text from Hank. He wants us to tap into a video call for an update."

Moe rose from the swing and pulled Breely to her feet. They'd had updates several times that week. They'd go to the war room and bring up the video conference software. Hank or Swede, or both, would appear and talk through what they'd learned. So far, all they'd done was knock names of potential suspects off the list. None of the names had come up in criminal databases or online news articles.

Swede and Kyla had promised to dig deeper. Moe translated that to mean hacking into bank and phone records of some of the people who'd been released from employment on the Brantt ranch.

Stone was first through the door into the war room. Kyla was on the computer, paging through data, determined to find something.

"Are you ready?" she asked.

"More than ready," Breely murmured. "Yes."

The big screen at the end of the conference table blinked. Hank and Swede appeared side by side.

"How are you holding up?" he asked.

"All is quiet here at the lodge," Moe said.

"Too quiet," Breely agreed. "What do you have?"

"Got information back on Cody West," Swede said.

Breely frowned and leaned forward. "What kind of information?"

"First of all, he's married with three kids, all under five years old," Hank said.

"Good for him," Breely said. "What does that have to do with me?"

"He's defaulted on his mortgage loan," Swede frowned. "The bank is foreclosing on his home in Bozeman."

"Again," Breely said, "what does that have to do with me?"

"Desperate times call for desperate measures," Swede said.

Hank picked up the narrative. "He has a strong motivation to do whatever it takes to save his family's home. No man wants his wife and three little kids kicked out into the street."

"That's not enough information to go after the man," Breely argued.

"No, but a twenty-thousand-dollar deposit to his checking account is a red flag. Enough to make the police question his whereabouts the night you were attacked," Hank said.

Breely pinched the bridge of her nose. "I remember Cody being a nice, respectful young man. Kidnapping a woman doesn't sound like something the Cody I knew would do. His only fault back then was getting involved with me. It got him kicked off the ranch."

Breely leaned forward. "Please, don't get the police involved...yet. If he's not the one, you're only making his crappy situation worse. Can't you send one of your guys out to question him? Hell, if you get me his phone number, I'll call him. He might not want to talk to me, but it's worth a try. My gut is telling me you're barking up the wrong tree. Do you have anything on any of the others on the list?"

"What about the Dillon guy who stole the money?" Moe asked.

"We've been looking into him, as well," Swede said. "His latest address is a mobile home park in Kalispell. We sent one of our guys up there to learn more. He got there yesterday and asked around. One of Dillon's friends said he recently purchased a bright yellow Corvette with a souped-up muffler. As the friend said, *It's bitchin'.* The same friend said Dillon had been hanging out with a guy from a local biker gang. They've been seen riding around together in the yellow Corvette—until a week ago."

Moe's gut twisted. This Dillon guy sounded like a winner.

Swede continued, "Dillon doesn't have much of a bank account. We don't see any sizable deposits, nor do we see any big withdrawals for a down payment on a car. We pulled his credit report. He doesn't have any current liens on a car or house. He declared bankruptcy six years ago. If he's driving a new Corvette, either he paid cash or he stole it."

Breely looked up at Hank and Swede. "Did your guy in Kalispell find Dillon?"

They shook their heads.

"No one has seen his yellow Corvette for over a week," Hank said. "No one saw it in Bozeman the night of your attack. The detective said the white van was found at an abandoned house on the outskirts of Bozeman. Someone could've hidden a flashy car there, used the van for the kidnapping then come back to his getaway car."

"It's been a week since the attack," Breely said. "If he was going to make a second attempt, wouldn't he have done it by now?"

Kyla waved a hand. "When could he?"

"Exactly. You've been surrounded by us, and you have a full-time bodyguard," Stone said. "That has to be putting a cramp in his plan."

"Has your father received any more death threats?" Kyla asked.

Breely shook her head. "No."

"I've been following the election campaign in Venezuela. Salazar is claiming DeVita is corrupt and that he's funneling drug money through the orphanages and community clinics the Brantt Philanthropy Foundation built to serve the people."

Breely nodded. "I'd heard. My people are launching a campaign to correct Salazar's claims.

They hope to reverse the damage Salazar's slur campaign has caused."

Kyla crossed her arms over her chest and gave Breely a devilish smile. "Despite spewing misinformation, DeVita is still ahead in the polls. He's projected to win."

"Which means Salazar has to be getting desperate," Hank said from the screen.

"Does Dillon and the kidnapping attempt have a connection to the Venezuelan election?" Breely shook her head. "I don't understand the point. I can see Dillon kidnapping me to extort money from my father. What does it have to do with anything else?"

"We checked with the detective in charge of the kidnapping investigation in Bozeman," Swede's lips twisted. "They don't have more information than they did a week ago."

"We need to find Dillon," Breely said.

"Before he finds Breely," Moe said.

"If he and his motorcycle gang sidekick are the kidnappers, they might have the answers we're looking for." Hank lifted his chin. "Be on the lookout for Dillon and or a bright yellow Corvette."

"We could use a current photo of him," Moe said.

"You know, I might have one." Breely pulled out her cell phone and scrolled through hundreds of photos. She slowed and eased through until she found what she was looking for. "Here." She handed her phone to Kyla.

Moe leaned over Kyla's shoulder.

Four men stood next to a corral fence, staring at the person taking the picture. "The guy on the right end is Dillon. Brown hair, brown eyes and same height as my father."

"Send the photo to us," Hank said.

Kyla waved a hand. "Will do."

"I'm going to tuck my kids in for their afternoon nap," Hank said. "Out here."

"Out here," Stone echoed.

The big screen went dark.

Stone turned to the others in the room. "Kyla will text Dillon's photo to our guys and Hank's team in Eagle Rock. Be vigilant."

"Headed back to the lodge?" Breely asked Stone.

He shook his head. "I'll stay here and work with Kyla to find out more about Dillon, where he bought his Corvette and how he paid for it.

Moe and Breely left the war room and returned to the lodge porch.

Moe lifted his glass of lemonade. "I could use a fresh glass. The ice is melted, and there's a bug in this one. You too?"

Breely nodded. "Yes. Then I want to call my father and catch up with them."

"Do we need to go back to our room to get your phone?" he asked.

Breely patted her back pocket. "No. Got it right here. We just need fresh drinks." She collected her glass and followed Moe through the lodge into the kitchen.

Cookie stood at the eight-burner gas stove, stirring something in a big stock pot.

Onion, garlic and chili pepper permeated the air.

Moe inhaled deeply. "Smells good, Cookie."

"Damn right it does. It's my prize-winning chili. It's what's for supper, along with jalapeño cornbread." He tipped his head toward the commercial refrigerator. "Lemonade is in the fridge."

"Thanks, Cookie." Breely took Moe's glass out of his hand, rinsed it and placed it in the dishwasher. She took another glass from the cupboard, put a couple of cubes of ice in it and added a cube to her glass.

Moe brought the pitcher of lemonade from the refrigerator and poured the liquid into the two glasses. When they were full, he returned the pitcher to the refrigerator. "Porch?"

Breely nodded.

Together, they walked out of the kitchen, through the open lobby toward the back porch.

Moe liked spending time with Breely. Sitting on the back porch, drinking lemonade might be boring to some, but he cherished the quiet times as much as the passionate ones.

In one week, he found himself falling hard for the pretty redhead. And he'd stopped fighting it. Yes, she was the client, but she was much more than that. She was a part of him, fully entrenched in his heart. He hadn't thought it would be possible to love again. Not after his first wife had left him.

Breely filled all the empty places in his soul. After only a week with the headstrong woman, who was as passionate about life as she was in bed, he couldn't imagine life without her.

"Do you mind taking my glass?" Breely held out her cup to Moe. "I need to use the facilities."

She turned and hurried to a short hallway where the restrooms were located, eager to return to the porch and Moe. As she passed the pretty alcove with the huge pot containing a massive, majestic palm, something moved between the thick layer of palm fronds.

Breely slowed and stared into the shadows created by the broad leaves. Whatever she'd thought had moved didn't move again.

She shrugged and moved on, pushing through the restroom's swinging door.

After relieving herself, she washed her hands and was drying them on a paper towel when a thunderous boom cracked the air and shook the floor so hard beneath her feet she clung to the counter to steady herself.

Dust and smoke drifted beneath the door into the bathroom.

What the hell had happened?

Where was Moe?

A sob rose in Breely's throat, strangling her vocal cords. She ran for the door, flung it open and stepped into a thick fog of dust that blinded her and filled her lungs.

She pulled her shirt over her mouth and nose then closed her eyes as much as she could and still see light.

Dull light.

The dust mixed with smoke was so thick she couldn't see two feet in front of her. She moved deliberately to her right until her hand touched the hallway wall. If she followed it to the end, she'd reached the lobby. And if she followed the other lobby wall, she'd eventually come to the door leading out onto the porch and clear, clean air.

And please, let Moe be there.

With her hand on the hallway wall, she shuffled her feet along the tile floor, moving slowly. If she lost the wall and ended up in the open space of the lobby, it would take her even longer to get outside.

The hallway wall took a sharp and unexpected detour. A wave of panic threatened to overwhelm Breely, but she couldn't give in to it. Not now. Not when she didn't know where Moe was or if any of the others had been caught in the explosion.

A waxy, smooth surface brushed against her hand, making her jump. Then she remembered the alcove and the huge plant, and she laughed at herself, coughing into her shirt. Touching her fingers gently to the palm fronds, she felt her way around the alcove until she found the hallway wall.

The sound of shuffling feet alerted her to the presence of someone else.

"Hey," she called out. "Can you hear me?"

"I can hear you," a muffled voice responded. A flashlight beam attempted to pierce the thick cloud only to be swallowed without providing sight of a way to cut through to the other side.

A hand clamped on her arm. In the shrouded mist of dust and smoke, a man wearing a worker's gray coverall and ball cap appeared in front of Breely. He had a kerchief tied around his face, covering his mouth and nose, and he wore goggles over his eyes. "Come with me," the muffled voice said. "I'll get you out."

Without waiting for her consent, he dragged her back the way she'd come. Down the hallway, past the restroom, he pulled her with one hand on her arm, the other on the wall.

After they'd gone several yards, Breely dug in her heels. "No." She coughed into her shirt. "Moe. Gotta get to Moe."

The hand on her arm tightened. "It's too dangerous. Let's get out this way and circle back."

He was right. The smoke had thickened, burning her lungs. She let the man lead her further down the hallway. If her memory was correct, there would be an emergency exit at the end.

When she thought her lungs could take no more, Breely heard the metal clank of the door lever being pushed. Then she was out of the lodge.

She sucked in a lungful of clean, clear air and coughed.

A gray pest control van stood in front of her, the side sliding door wide open.

Breely turned and started for the side of the lodge, her only focus on getting to Moe. She hoped he'd gone out on the porch and not back to the kitchen.

She only made it two steps before the man in the gray coveralls blocked her path.

He didn't say a word, just stood there,

"Move," she demanded and coughed, the smoke and dust she'd inhaled making her voice coarse. Her eyes watered and stung. She blinked to clear them.

Coverall man grabbed her arms.

Breely tried to knock his hands away.

His grip tightened.

She backed away and ran into a wall.

Only it wasn't a wall. It was another man. His arm wrapped around her, trapping her arms to her sides. A meaty hand clamped over her mouth. He lifted her and carried her toward the van.

"No!" Her cry was muffled beneath the sweaty

palm. The nightmare of her previous encounter with two men and a van unfolded in front of her.

Breely fought with every ounce of strength she had, kicking and twisting.

The man who'd blocked her path grabbed her ankles.

Together, the men climbed into the van with her. The one holding her feet released his hold, slammed the van door closed and dove into the driver's seat.

The guy behind her flipped her onto her stomach and pressed his knee into her back.

With her chest smashed into the metal floor of the van and the big man leaning hard into her spine, Breely couldn't move...couldn't...breathe.

She tried to buck and roll, but the man's weight kept her pinned.

The vehicle lurched forward and increased speed, carrying her away from the lodge. Away the Brotherhood Protectors. Away from Moe.

Tears leaked out of the corners of her eyes. She couldn't give up. In the chaos of the explosion, they wouldn't know she was missing. How long would it take Moe to realize she was gone?

Any amount of time was too long as the van put more and more distance between her and Moe.

He wouldn't be there to rescue her this time. She'd have to get herself out of this situation—which meant focusing.

She studied what she could see around her, hoping to locate something she could use as a weapon. There were hoses and plastic containers filled with pesticides. Surely, she could make something work.

First, she had to get the man off her back. Fighting hadn't dislodged him. His weight pressing down on her wasn't making it easy for her to get air into her lungs. If she didn't get out from under him soon, she'd pass out.

Breely stopped fighting, closed her eyes and went limp. If he thought she'd passed out, the big guy on top of her might move away.

She lay for a long time, praying the man would move.

For her plan to work, the big guy had to notice she'd passed out.

If he didn't move soon…she *would* lose consciousness from lack of air.

CHAPTER 12

MOE HAD SET the two glasses of lemonade on a table next to the porch swing when the explosion ripped through the peace and quiet, shaking the timbers beneath his feet.

Smoke billowed out of the southern end of the lodge.

Moe raced back toward the door he'd just come through. When he opened it, smoke and dust wrapped around him, making him cough. He dragged his T-shirt over his face and stepped into the foggy haze that had been the beautiful, light-filled lobby.

Unable to see past the nose on his face, Moe turned to his left and touched his hand to the wall. Moving slowly, he felt his way around the room, bumping into end tables, easing around couches and chairs and running into display signs.

Though he kept hunkered low, the smoke burned his eyes and lungs. Still, he pushed forward, cursing how slow he had to move, knowing he didn't have time to waste. He had to get to Breely and get her out of the lodge before smoke inhalation claimed her.

When he finally made it to the hallway where the restrooms were located, he pushed through the door of the ladies' room. Inside, the smoke and haze weren't as thick. It didn't take long to check all the stalls.

His heart sank to his knees. Breely wasn't there.

Back out into the thickening smoke, Moe didn't know where to begin. "Breely!" he called out through the fabric of his shirt.

He strained to listen for her response.

Had she run out into the lobby, gotten confused and collapsed due to smoke inhalation? Or had she headed for the nearest exit?

She was a smart woman. She'd get out through the nearest door.

He remembered the emergency exit at the end of the hallway and worked his way toward it. With one hand on the wall, the other in front of him, he ran until his hand hit the wall at the end of the hall. He pushed against the door lever and burst out into the open.

Moe dragged air into his lungs and scanned the area for Breely. She wasn't there.

He ran around the side of the building toward the front of the lodge.

Nothing moved in the parking lot. Breely wasn't there.

On the street beyond, a gray pest control van drove past as if nothing was wrong when, in fact, things had just gone to shit.

Where was Breely?

Moe raced back around the lodge to the rear, hoping Breely had come out that direction and was looking for him.

Stone and Kyla ran up from the barn. Tinker and John Jacobs raced up from the direction of one of the storage buildings.

Moe met them near the back porch.

"What happened?" Stone asked.

"There was an explosion," Moe coughed. "I can't find Breely."

"Where was she the last time you saw her?" Kyla asked.

He tilted his head toward the lodge. "She'd gone to the restroom."

When Kyla started for the entrance, Moe caught her arm. "I checked. She's not in there."

"The smoke and fire seem to be coming from the kitchen," John said. "What about Cookie?"

"Sweet Jesus." Kyla took off running.

They raced to the end of the building where the

kitchen was located in time to see Cookie stumble through the kitchen door and drop to his knees, coughing and hacking.

Moe rushed to him. "Was Breely with you when the explosion happened?"

Cookie shook his head and coughed harder. "Last I…saw her…she was …with you."

Sirens wailed in the distance, growing louder.

"Is there anyone else in the building," Kyla asked.

Stone's eyes narrowed. "Our team is all out for the day."

John shook his head. "All the guests either checked out this morning or headed out to Yellowstone for the day. Shouldn't be anyone inside."

"Except Breely," Moe started for the door.

Stone grabbed his arm. "It's too smoky."

Moe strained against Stone's hold. "Let go. I need to get her out."

"Does she have her phone on her?" Kyla asked.

Moe nodded. "In her back pocket."

"Didn't you put a phone locator app on yours and hers?" Kyla asked.

"Yes!" Moe dug his cell phone out of his back pocket and clicked on the phone finder app. If he knew exactly where she was, he might get to her faster.

The app brought up a map of West Yellowstone with a blue dot indicating his location and a circle with Breely's tiny image pinpointing her position.

Moe cursed. "She's not here."

"What do you mean?" Stone leaned over Moe's shoulder.

"She's not in the lodge. She's on Canyon Street headed north."

"Toward the airport," John Jacobs said.

"I'm calling the sheriff." Stone stepped away and dialed 911.

Moe's heart squeezed hard. How had he failed her so badly? He looked around. "I have to get there. If they put her on a plane…"

"Can you handle a dirt bike?" John Jacobs asked.

Moe nodded. "Raced them as a teen back in South Dakota."

"Take my dirt bike," John said.

"I'll get it." Tinker raced down the hill to a storage building.

Moe shook his head. "They have too big a head start."

"You can go the back way," John said. "Give me your phone." He traced a thin line on the map. "That's a dirt road. It'll get you there faster. It just isn't good for cars, but the motorcycle will handle it."

With hope swelling in his chest, Moe took off after Tinker.

An engine roared from the metal building. A moment later, Tinker blasted around the side on a bike that had to have been used racing in motocross. He stopped beside Moe and leaped off.

Moe hopped on, hit the throttle and headed down the highway leading northwest out of town. Not far past the edge of West Yellowstone, he turned onto the dirt road John had shown him on the map. It was bumpy, full of potholes and overgrown with weeds and brush.

Moe hadn't ridden a dirt bike in a decade. It bounced and jerked as it hit rough patches but handled the uneven terrain. Better than Moe did.

The dirt road intersected with another dirt road that ran parallel to the airport runway. This road was straight and more even than the previous road.

Moe opened up the throttle, leaned over the bike and flew like the wind.

Ahead, a spec in the sky got bigger, heading toward the north end of the airport. The closer it came, the better Moe could make out what it was.

A helicopter.

From what Moe remembered, the helicopter pad was near the smoke-jumper school at the north end of the airport.

The helicopter approached the airport and hovered over the pad.

Moe had the bike at full throttle. He could make it go faster but still wouldn't get there before the helicopter that was slowly lowering to the ground.

As he neared the airport terminal area, he left the dirt road and turned into the parking lot where he'd picked up his rental car. At that moment, a maintenance vehicle passed through a gate, and the gate was closing slowly behind him.

Moe hit the throttle, swerved around the maintenance truck and raced out onto the tarmac.

The helicopter's skids were just touching the ground, the length of the runway away.

What looked like a gray van drove past the fire training area, heading for the chopper.

Moe pushed the bike as fast as it would go. It wasn't fast enough.

The van stopped short of the helicopter blades. The side door slid open. A blur of movement exploded out the door.

Red hair whipped in the wind as Breely darted away from the van and the helicopter.

Two men raced after her.

She ran at least thirty yards before the thinner man tackled her to the ground and held her there until the big guy caught up. Together, they lifted her between them.

Rage burned inside Moe. Just a little further.

His time was running out. The men had Breely and were heading to the helicopter.

Moe was fifty yards away when the men reached the chopper. As they tried to get inside with Breely, she bucked and twisted.

The thinner guy stumbled, dropped his hold on

Breely's legs and fell to the ground. He was up in a second, reaching for Breely's legs.

She kicked out, catching the man in the chin and sending him flying backward.

When he came back at Breely, he backhanded her across her face.

Her head snapped to the right, and she lay still.

Moe's hands tightened on the handlebars. He'd kill the guy for hurting Breely.

The men lifted her up and into the helicopter.

As they scrambled in behind her, Moe reached the helipad, driving up from the rear of the aircraft.

He raced straight for the open side door.

As he came alongside, the chopper started to rise into the air.

Moe flung himself off the bike and in through the open doorway, landing on top of the bigger man who'd been struggling to get to his feet.

He knocked the big guy flat on his belly.

Breely lay on the floor beside him, her eyes closed.

The helicopter rocked, hovering a few feet from the ground.

The skinnier guy cocked his leg and swung his foot straight at Moe's head.

Moe rolled in time to avoid the man's boot.

As the foot whizzed past his ear, Moe grabbed the man's leg, twisted and shoved him backward.

He fell, landing hard against the other door.

The big guy beneath Moe bucked.

Moe rolled off him and let the man get to his knees. As the man was pushing to his feet, Moe kicked hard, landing his boots in the man's side with enough force to launch him backward. He staggered a few feet. The helicopter pitched to the starboard. The big man teetered, arms flailing wildly and fell out.

Moe leaped to his feet.

The other man pushed himself upright and lunged at Moe. Bigger and heavier than Moe, he had the advantage of weight.

Moe had the advantage of agility.

The man swung his fist.

Moe swayed right, grabbed the arm and twisted it up and around, jamming it high between the man's shoulder blades.

Below him, Breely stirred and pushed to her feet. Her eyes widened when she saw Moe with her captor subdued.

She glanced around, grabbed a headset and yanked the cord out of the socket. Then she leaned over the back of the pilot's seat, looped the cord around his neck and pulled tight. "Land! Now!" she yelled over the roar of the engine.

The pilot rocked the craft, trying to throw Breely off balance. She only pulled tighter.

Finally, the pilot lowered the helicopter, landing in the middle of the runway.

Once on the ground, she shouted into the pilot's ear. "Shut it down! Now!"

The pilot hit switches, the engine noise died and the rotors slowed to a halt.

Within seconds, the craft was completely surrounded by airport security, sheriff's vehicles, fire trucks, an ambulance and Stone's black SUV.

Brotherhood Protectors piled out and ran toward the chopper. Kyla ran the other direction toward the big man Moe had pushed out of the door.

Sheriff's deputies pointed their weapons at the helicopter as Moe pushed his guy toward the door. He shoved hard and released the man's arm at the same time.

The guy dropped to the ground, stumbled and fell to his knees.

Moe held up his hands.

Breely stepped up beside him, her hands in the air. "Don't let the pilot get away," she called out.

The sheriff motioned for Moe and Breely to get out of the helicopter.

Deputies leaped in and secured the pilot.

"Sheriff Hartsell." John Jacobs approached the sheriff, pointed at Moe and Breely, whose hands were still in the air, and said, "They're the good guys."

"You sure?" The sheriff's eyes narrowed on Moe.

"Positive. Moe works for my son and the Brotherhood Protectors. The pretty one is Breely Brantt, Robert Brantt's daughter. You might not want to point that gun at her. If it goes off, you'll have a helluva a lot to explain to her father."

The sheriff turned his weapon toward the man kneeling on the ground. One of his deputies had secured the man's wrists behind his back. "And who is this?"

Breely walked around to stand in front of the brown-haired man. "Dillon Sarley. He worked for my father until he was caught stealing money out of my father's office. Daddy never should've let you slide. You should've gone to jail back then."

"He's a stupid, gullible man," Dillon snarled. "He didn't need the money. He's loaded."

"And you needed the money to buy a fancy Corvette?" Breely shook her head. "How did you pay for it? You got it before you could ransom me."

He snorted. "I wasn't going to ransom you. I got paid a butt load just to get you on this helicopter."

Moe stood beside Breely. "Who paid you?"

Dillon spat at Moe's boots. "Why should I tell you?"

"Why shouldn't you?" Moe cocked an eyebrow.

Dillon shrugged. "I prefer to live."

"I hope you enjoy life in jail," Moe said. "It's not any safer there than out here. And if the right rumor is spread, the prisoners will make sure certain people are taken care of."

Dillon's eyes narrowed.

"I don't care either way." Moe slipped his arm

around Breely. "Salazar's going to lose the election. The cartel will cut his funding, and he'll either be run out of Venezuela or killed."

Dillon shook his head. "I don't know what you're talking about."

"You're not going to get a plea bargain," a voice said behind Moe.

Kyla joined them. Behind her, a gurney was being loaded into the back of the ambulance, "You're friend was quick to tell the deputy everything he knew. Said he wasn't keen on kidnapping no woman for some South American dictator, but the money was good." Kyla grinned. "He also said you were only paying him a tenth of what you stood to make. You bought a Corvette with the first installment. Your buddy only got enough to pay off the loan on his Harley."

"Asshole," Dillon muttered. "He doesn't know anything. He's just a dumb biker."

Kyla crossed her arms over her chest and stared down her nose at Dillon. "That dumb biker overheard you talking to some dude with an accent about kidnapping the girl and taking her down to Venezuela. They'd threaten to kill her if her father didn't make a public announcement about using his orphanages and community health centers to funnel drugs through Venezuela and into the US. Plus, he'd have to claim that he'd used drug money to fund DeVita's campaign."

Breely shook her head. "You got all that out of the guy who fell out of a helicopter?"

"Pain has a way of making a guy talk. Not that I was the cause of the pain. The bones he broke upon landing were enough." Kyla gave Breely a cocky shrug. "I'm just that good at questioning. I make them want to tell me things."

Breely laughed. "You're amazing. I want to be like you someday."

Kyla's brow dipped. "No. You don't. Unless you like the part where I have a man who loves me despite my past and body count."

Moe stared down at Breely. "You've got that."

"Which part?" Breely stared up at him, her eyes wide. "The body count or the love?"

"Love. All the way." He kissed the top of her head.

The deputies brought the pilot out of the helicopter, his wrists secured with zip ties behind his back. He and Dillon were placed in the backs of two different sheriff's SUVs.

Moe looked down at Breely, his heart so full he felt it might explode. He couldn't wait to get her somewhere he could hold her close and tell her how he really felt. Having almost lost her, he realized she was so much more than a job or a friend. "Ready?"

She wrapped her arm around his waist. "I sure am. But where are we going? The lodge was full of smoke." Her eyes widened. "The lodge! Did everyone get out?"

John Jacobs spoke up. "I was on the phone with Tinker. There's smoke damage, and where Dillon and his cohort set the explosion, a wall needs to be rebuilt. It'll be a massive cleanup effort."

"I'm so sorry," Breely said. "I'll do what I can to help with the cleanup. I'm pretty good at cleaning."

"What's important is that no one was severely hurt," Stone said. "The lodge will survive."

Tinker joined them, pushing the dirt bike along the runway toward them. "Just a couple of scratches. It still works," he reported with a grin.

Moe glanced down at Breely. "Wanna ride back on the bike?"

Her eyes brightened. "Can we?"

Tinker shrugged. "Don't see why not."

Moe nodded to Stone. "See you back at the lodge." He slung his leg over the bike and scooted forward.

Breely climbed onto the back and wrapped her arms around his waist. "Another adventure. And the best part about it is how close I get to be to you."

Moe started the engine and drove the dirt bike off the runway and through the gate.

He loved how Breely fit perfectly against his body and in his life.

Taking it a little slower on the way back, he showed her how much fun riding through life with him could be.

He hoped she would consider making it permanent.

Yeah, the man who'd thought he never wanted to marry again had fallen hard. He couldn't imagine anything better than having this redhead by his side for the rest of his life.

EPILOGUE

Two months later...

Moe held the door for Breely as they stepped out the back door of the lodge carrying glasses of iced lemonade.

Breely laughed. "I feel a little déjà vu, don't you?" A shiver rippled down her spine despite the bright summer sunshine warming the air in West Yellowstone. "I can't believe it's been two months since the explosion."

Moe nodded. "Thankfully, Dillon is behind bars along with his sidekick."

"Between the sidekick and the pilot, they filled in the blanks. Dillon didn't have to tell all." Breely sighed. "I think it's fitting that we're celebrating the lodge reopening today and that Venezuela is electing a new president. I can't wait to find out who won."

"Me, too." Moe glanced over his shoulder. "Are they coming?"

"I thought they were." Breely leaned back into the lodge. "Mom, Dad, are you coming out back with us?"

"We're coming," her mother said. "Your father filled his glass too full and is afraid he'll spill it on the freshly cleaned floors."

Moe held the door for Breely's folks.

Her mother patted his cheek on her way through. "You're a good man, Morris."

Breely was glad her mother and father had warmed up to Moe. She loved her parents and wanted them to love the man she cared about most. And Breely loved Moe with all her heart.

Everything about that day was beautiful and good. Breely was happy that all of Moe's team were able to make the celebratory reopening of the lodge. Their girlfriends and fiancées had come as well.

Stone and John Jacobs had grill duty, with strict instructions from Cookie not to burn the steaks.

Cookie had recovered nicely from smoke inhalation and was busy in the kitchen with Tinker as his helper, making all the sides that would accompany the meats on the grill.

Tables had been arranged on the back porch, with red gingham tablecloths and vases of red and white carnations. That had been Breely's mother's contribution. Fiona Brantt had fallen in love with the lodge and West Yellowstone the moment she'd arrived a week ago.

Robert Brantt had pulled strings and called in favors to have the lodge restored in record time. He'd even had a stone pizza oven built in the place where the explosion had blown out a wall in the kitchen.

If Cookie hadn't been in the pantry when the charges had gone off, he wouldn't have survived. The kitchen had been demolished.

Breely's father had worked with his architects and John Jacobs to have the place restored with all the modern conveniences and an eye to preserving the structural past. Both John and Cookie had been thrilled with the outcome.

An army of restoration specialists had cleaned the walls, ceilings and wood floors, removing soot and the smell. Carpets and furniture that couldn't be salvaged had been replaced.

Breely had just set down her glass of lemonade when the back door of the lodge opened and a German shepherd trotted through, followed by two women and two more men.

One of the women Breely recognized by the advertisements and movie trailers. Her beautiful light blond hair and blue eyes were unmistakable.

Breely recognized the man with her as Hank Patterson, the one who'd been with Moe at the

Tumbleweed Tavern the night that had changed her life.

Hank leaned close to his wife. "Darling, I think we timed it right. I smell steak!"

"Of course, you smell it. We sent some of our best down for this celebration." She crossed the porch to where Kyla leaned against a post, her face pale. "Kyla, honey, it's so good to see you."

Kyla gave her a wan smile but held up her hands. "Great to see you too, Sadie, and I'd love a hug, but you might not want to get too close."

Sadie frowned, "Why?"

Kyla rubbed her belly. "I'm not feeling too hot, today. I think it's something I ate."

"Oh, sweetie," Sadie took her arm and led her to a rocking chair. "You sit and let everyone else help themselves. Would you like for me to get you a glass of ginger ale to help settle your stomach?"

Kyla shook her head. "No, thank you. Really, I'll be fine. I don't want to bring this party down over a little tummy disagreement."

"You're not bringing us down." Sadie made her way around the porch and out onto the lawn greeting everyone. Her smile made each person feel like her best friend.

When she came back up to the porch, she stopped in front of Breely. "I hear you're going to work at the lodge."

Breely nodded. "I love being around people and

close to Moe and his team. Mr. Jacobs said that I could bring my horse down from Kalispell if I want. They have room in the barn."

Sadie hugged her close. "I'm just glad you've decided to stay with us. You're part of the family." She glanced over at Moe. "Has he made it official yet?"

Breely's cheeks heated. "We're happy. What more do we need?"

Sadie nodded. "He hasn't asked."

"Sadie," Hank caught her arm, "are you match-making again? Leave these people alone. They need to do things in their own time."

Hank grimaced at Breely. "My wife thinks everyone should be married with at least two babies."

"Happily married," Sadie corrected. "I wish everyone could be as happy as I am with you, Hank."

He smiled down at his wife and bent to brush his lips across hers. "And I'm crazy, stupid in love with you, my dear."

Breely's heart swelled at the love unashamedly displayed between Hank and Sadie.

Hank straightened. "Breely, Robert, Fiona, have you met Kujo, Molly and Six?"

Breely shook her head and turned to the tall man with black hair and blue eyes. "Kujo?"

The man held out his hand. "Joseph Kuntz. Kuntz, Joseph. KuJo." He shook her hand. "They gave the handle in Army Basic Combat Training, and it's been with me ever since."

Kujo shook hands with Breely's parents and Moe. "Welcome aboard, man. He turned to the woman beside him whose belly was the size of a watermelon. "This is my wife, Molly."

Breely took the woman's hand, surprised at the strength of her grip. "Stone was telling me you're an FBI special agent."

Molly nodded, her hand rubbing across her belly. "I am. Though I will be going on maternity leave soon."

"Congratulations," Breely hugged her. She bent to the dog at Molly's feet. "And who do we have here?"

"This is Six." Molly's hand smoothed over the dog's head. "He's the retired Military Working Dog Kujo trained when he was on active duty."

"He's beautiful." Breely smiled and looked for Moe.

He was close by, leaning on the porch rail. His gaze shifted to the sky then to her. He stood with his hand in his pocket, but he wasn't relaxed or at ease. Again, he glanced up at the sky. Why was he looking weird? It was like he was anxious or nervous.

Breely went to him and laid a hand on his chest. "Hey. Are you okay?"

"Sure," he said, looking up at the sky again.

Breely shook her head. "You're not okay. What's wrong?"

He smiled down at her. "Nothing, sweetheart. Nothing at all." Again, he glanced at the sky and then back to her.

Breely looked up. The sky was a beautiful summertime blue. "Are you sure you're feeling all right?"

He tugged at the collar of his button-down shirt. "Never felt better."

"Do you need a ginger ale to settle your stomach?" she asked.

"Huh?" He looked at her quizzically then shook his head. "No."

"Then could you get me another lemonade?" she asked.

He frowned. "No. I can't."

Breely tilted her head. "What the heck is wrong with you?"

He glanced at the sky again, a smile spreading across his face. "Come with me, and I'll tell you what's wrong with me." He took her hand and led her down the porch steps and out onto the lawn. "Look up, Breely."

"Huh? I thought you were going to tell me what was wrong with you."

He nudged her chin with a finger and pointed to the sky. "Look up, my love."

Breely glanced up in time to see a plane fly over dragging a long banner behind it.

She squinted and shaded her eyes against the

sun. "Breely... Hey, it has my name on it." She looked again. "I can't quite read it. What does it say?"

"Oh, good grief," Kyla said from the porch. "It says, *Breely, Will You Marry Me?* Moe, get down on your knee, for God's sake." Kyla's face paled, and she leaned over the porch rail and vomited.

Sadie rushed to the woman, slipped her arm around her and led her to the door. "Don't stop on our account. We'll be back." She disappeared inside with Kyla. Stone started to follow.

Hank gripped his arm. "Let Sadie handle it. Your teammate is in the middle of a proposal."

"He is?" Breely turned back to Moe.

He wasn't standing in front of her but was on one knee, looking up at her.

"You are?" Breely squeaked.

"I am," he said with a smile. "Breely Brantt, I love you so much I can't breathe without you. Would you do me the great honor of becoming my wife, so I can love you for the rest of my life?"

Tears filled Breely's eyes. She dropped to her knees in front of him. "Yes! Oh, yes! I would be the happiest woman that ever lived to be your wife." She flung her arms around his neck and kissed him.

Thunderous applause sounded all around them with cheering and shouts of congratulations.

Moe stood and swung Breely up into his arms. "You all heard it. She said yes. We're getting married!"

For the next ten minutes, Breely was hugged by every person there.

John and Stone pulled the steaks off the grill and carried them to the tables. As everyone found a seat, Sadie came out of the lodge with Kyla, sporting a huge grin on her face. Kyla's expression was more one of shell shock.

"Did she say yes?" Sadie asked.

Moe answered, "Yes."

"Oh, good. Congratulations, you two." She turned to Kyla and pulled her up to stand beside her. "We have more good news." She paused. "Where's Stone?"

Stone hurried over to stand with Kyla. "What's the good news?"

Sadie turned to Kyla. "You tell him."

Kyla looked up into Stone's face. "This is one mission I'm not at all prepared for." She raised her hand. In it was a wand. "Honey, we're pregnant."

Stone's face blanched white. "What? Are you kidding? How?"

Kyla laughed. "Pregnant. No kidding. And you know how." She stared up at him. "Are you okay with this?"

Stone cupped her cheeks between his palms. "Okay? I'm more than okay. I love you, Kyla. I can't wait to start this new adventure with a family."

More congratulations went around before everyone settled at the tables.

Moe leaned over to Breely. "We never talked about kids. How do you feel about kids?"

"I love them and want half a dozen."

Moe let go of a breath he'd been holding. "Me, too. I know it's just happened, but what are you thinking about a date for our wedding and where?"

"How does next weekend in Vegas sound?" she whispered.

"Like heaven," he said. "I'd like to get started on those dozen children before I'm too old to enjoy them."

She squeezed his leg under the table. "I love you, Morris Cleveland. And I love that you proposed with a plane. I can't wait to be your wife and fly off into the sunset with my very own pararescue pilot."

Moe kissed the tip of her nose. "And I can't wait to marry my redhaired beauty and start our own happily ever after."

DRAKE

IRON HORSE LEGACY BOOK #6

New York Times & *USA Today*
Bestselling Author

ELLE JAMES

DRAKE

IRON HORSE LEGACY

New York Times & *USA Today* Bestselling Author

ELLE JAMES

CHAPTER 1

"DAMN," Drake Morgan muttered, checked his speedometer and repeated the expletive.

He hadn't realized he'd been going over the sixty-miles-an-hour speed limit until blue lights flashed in his rearview mirror. Lifting his foot off the accelerator, he slowed and eased to the side of the road, just a few miles from his destination.

A county sheriff's SUV pulled to a stop behind him, and a deputy dropped down from the driver's seat.

The tan, short-sleeved uniform shirt stretched taut over full breasts, the shirt-tails tucked into the waistband of dark brown trousers, cinched around a narrow waist with a thick black belt.

Definitely female. Too petite and pretty to be out patrolling the wild roads of rural Montana.

He lowered the window of his Ford F250 pickup,

reached into his glove box for the vehicle registration and insurance information she'd surely request and straightened.

"Sir, place your hands on the window frame," she said.

He raised his hands, one of which held the documents. The other he carefully placed on the window frame of his door, staring out the open window into the barrel of a pistol. He raised his gaze to the deputy's and cocked an eyebrow. "I have a concealed carry license," he warned. "My weapon is in the glove compartment. I'm unarmed at this moment."

"Just keep your hands where I can see them," she said, her tone curt, her eyes narrowed as she held the pistol pointed at his head.

"Can I ask why I was pulled over?" he asked in a calm, even tone, knowing the answer.

"You were exceeding the speed limit," she said. "If that's your title and registration, I'll take those. But no funny business."

"Trust me," he said with a crooked smile. "I've never been accused of being funny."

Her eyebrows pulled together to form a V over her nose as she took the papers he held out for her.

She studied the documents then glanced up. "You're not from around here," she said.

"No, I'm not," he said.

"Do you know how fast you were going?" she asked, all business, no smile.

Drake almost grinned at the seriousness of the young woman's expression and the way she stiffly held herself. "Over the speed limit?"

She snorted. "By at least fifteen miles an hour. In a hurry to get somewhere?"

"I was."

She shook her head, a hint of a smile tugging at the corners of her mouth. "And how's that working out for you?"

"You tell me," he quipped.

She was pretty in a girl-next-door kind of way with light brown hair pulled back in an efficient ponytail.

Drake stared up into her eyes, trying to decide if they were brown, gold or green, finally settling on hazel. To cap it all, she sported a dusting of freckles on her bare face. "You have my information, but let me introduce myself." He stuck out his hand. "Drake Morgan."

Her brow furrowed as she contemplated his extended hand. "I'm Deputy Douglas." She gave a brief nod, ignored his hand and stared past him into the vehicle. "Since you have a gun in the vehicle with you, you'll need to step out of the truck while I run your data."

Already late for the meeting with his team, their new boss, and this his first day on the job, he sighed, pushed open the door and stepped out with his hands held high.

"Turn around, place your hands on the hood of your vehicle and spread your legs," she said in a tone that brooked no argument.

He cocked an eyebrow. "I'm not a convicted felon. I owned up to the gun in my glove box. I'm unarmed and at your mercy."

Having stated her demand once, she held the gun pointed at his chest, unbending, waiting for him to follow through.

Rather than give her a reason to pull the trigger, he turned and complied with her command.

The shuffle of gravel indicated she'd moved closer. A small, capable hand skimmed over his shoulders, down his sides, around to his abs and lower. Bypassing his private parts, her hand traveled the length of his legs, patting both all the way to his ankles.

Out of the corner of his eye, he watched as she balanced her service weapon with her right hand as she frisked him with her left.

Finally, she straightened and stepped back. "Please stand at the rear of your vehicle while I run your plates and license."

He turned and gave her a twisted grin. "Told you I was unarmed."

She backed toward her vehicle then slipped into the driver's seat. Her fingers danced across a computer keyboard as she entered his license and registration data and waited.

Moments later, she got out of her work vehicle, weapon back in the holster on her belt, and strode toward him while writing on an official-looking pad. When she reached him, she ripped off the top sheet and handed it to him. "I'm only giving you a warning this time. Next time, I'll cite you. Slow it down out there. The life you endanger might not be your own."

With that parting comment, she spun on her booted heels and marched back to her vehicle.

"Deputy Douglas," he called out.

As she opened her SUV, she turned to face him, "Yes, Mr. Morgan?"

"You're the first person I've met here. Nice to meet you." He waved the warning ticket. "And thank you."

Her brow furrowed, and she shook her head as she climbed into the vehicle. Moments later, she passed his truck and continued toward the little town of Eagle Rock ahead of him.

Drake slipped into the driver's seat and followed at a more sedate pace. Hell, he was already late. What were a few more minutes? And it wasn't worth getting a full-fledged ticket. He was lucky she'd only issued a warning. She could've hit him hard with a speeding ticket, with the lasting effect of jacking up his insurance rates.

He owed her a coffee or a beer. Since she was the only person from Eagle Rock he knew besides Hank Patterson, he'd kind of like to get to know her better.

It paid to have the law on your side in these backwater towns.

Following the GPS map on his dash, he drove through town and out the other end, turning on the road leading to his destination.

Soon, he saw her, perched on the side of a mountain, her broad porches intact, her late eighteen-hundred charm shining through, despite the need for a good paint job and dry-rot repair.

The Lucky Lady Lodge clung to the side of the mountain, welcoming travelers in search of a quiet getaway in the Crazy Mountains of Montana.

From what Hank had told him, this lodge had been a place for the gold rush miners of the late eighteen hundreds to spend their hard-earned gold on booze and women.

After the gold had dried up, the Lucky Lady had become a speakeasy during the prohibition, with secret passages into the old mine where they'd made moonshine and stored the contraband in the mountain.

Drake had done some research on the old lodge. He'd found stories telling of days when mafia kingpins had come to conduct business while hunting in the hills or fishing in the mountain streams.

Fires had consumed hundreds of acres surrounding the lodge, missing it on more than one occasion by less than a mile. Throughout the years, the lodge stood as she had from the beginning, a little worn around the edges. Recently, she'd been damaged by an explosion in the mine. That's where Drake and his team would come in.

He looked forward to rolling up his sleeves and putting his carpentry skills to work restoring the old girl. He hoped that, like riding a bike, it would all come back to him despite the sixteen years it had been since he'd last lifted a hammer to build or repair anything more than a deck on the house of a friend. The summers he'd spent working on new home construction while in high school gave him skills he wouldn't have known otherwise and the confidence to try new things he'd never done.

Having joined the Navy straight out of high school, he hadn't had much need for carpentry skills. He'd focused all his attention on being the best military guy he could be. That had meant working his ass off and applying for the elite Navy SEALs training.

BUD/S had been the most difficult training he'd ever survived. Once he'd made it through, he'd been deployed on a regular basis to all corners of the world, fighting wars he thought were to help people who couldn't help themselves or protect his own country from the tyranny of others.

Drake snorted. He'd learned all too soon that war wasn't always for just causes. When he'd tired of putting his life on the line for the benefit of big business, he'd said goodbye to what had been the only career he'd ever wanted.

From there, he'd worked with Stone Jacobs as a mercenary in Afghanistan, leaving just in time before the US pulled out and left Stone and the last five members of his team stranded.

Rumor had it that former SEAL, Hank Patterson, had sent a rescue team to get Jacobs and his people out.

Since Afghanistan, Drake had refused to be another hired mercenary. He'd been drifting from one low-paying job to another. Nothing seemed to fit.

When Hank Patterson had called him out of the blue, he'd been working at a small diner in the backwoods of East Texas, dissatisfied with life, unable to fit into the civilian world and ready for any change that would take him away from the diner, the small-minded residents of the town and the meddling mamas bent on matching their single daughters to the only bachelor in town with all of his original teeth.

No, thank you.

Drake had been ready to leave East Texas.

When Hank's call had come, he'd been willing to listen and even come to Montana for a one-on-one chat with his old friend and brother-in-arms.

Hank had offered Drake a job as a Brotherhood Protector, a kind of security firm providing protection, extraction and whatever else was warranted for people who needed the expertise of someone skilled in special operations.

"I'm not interested in mercenary work," Drake had said. "Been there...done that."

"It's not mercenary work," Hank had said. "It's bodyguard, rescue and protective services for real people who need specialized help. We aren't working for big corporations."

Drake had been insistent. "Not interested. Got anything else?"

Hank chuckled. "As a matter of fact, I know someone who needs carpenters for a lodge restoration project. It's good physical work, and the lodge is worth restoring."

"Sounds more my speed," Drake said.

"Come out to Montana. See what we have here and make your decision," Hank had urged.

Drake had remained firm. "I'm not going to change my mind."

"Okay. I get it. But I want you to meet the guys who work with me and get their take on what we do."

"Fair enough," Drake said. "I'd still rather pound nails. It beats slinging bullets."

"I'll put you in touch with Molly McKinnon and Parker Bailey. They are leading the effort to restore the lodge. I've sent several spec ops guys their way already. You probably know some of them or know of them."

"I'm down for some renovation work with a team

full of former spec ops guys, as long as they aren't going to try to talk me into working for your Brotherhood Protectors." He thought he might have insulted Hank. "No offense."

Hank laughed. "None taken. Whichever way you lean in the job front, you'll love Montana and the little town of Eagle Rock."

Anything would be better than the close-minded, stone-faced inhabitants of the small East Texas town he'd worked in for the past six months.

"How soon can you get here?" Hank asked. "The other four SEALs are due to start on Monday morning."

"I'll be there," Drake had assured him.

"Great. See you then," Hank ended the call.

Drake had immediately given the diner his resignation, packed up his few personal items in his furnished apartment and left Texas. He'd driven for two days, stopping only long enough to catch a couple of hours of sleep at a rest area along the way.

When he rolled to a stop in the parking lot in front of the Lucky Lady Lodge, with the Crazy Mountains as a backdrop to the old building, he already felt more at home than he had anywhere else. Maybe it was because he was tired. More likely, he felt that way because he didn't want to move again.

As he stepped down from his pickup, he shrugged off his exhaustion. He could sink his teeth into this project. It beat cleaning years of grease off the diner's floor back in Texas.

With a new sense of purpose, he passed the large roll-on-roll-off trash bin, already half-full of broken boards, crumbled sheets of drywall panels, ruined carpet and damaged furniture. He climbed the steps to the wide veranda and entered through the stately double doors of the lodge.

Six men and a woman stood in the lobby, wearing jeans and T-shirts. They had gathered around a drafting table, all looking down at what appeared to be blueprints.

The woman glanced up. "Oh, good. Drake's here."

The others straightened and turned toward Drake.

As he studied the faces, his heart filled with joy.

He knew Hank from way back at the beginning of his career as a Navy SEAL. Hank had been the experienced SEAL who'd taken him under his wing and shown him the ropes of what it was like beyond BUD/S. Clean-shaven, he had a short haircut, unlike the shaggy look he'd acquired on active duty. The man had a few more wrinkles around his green eyes, but he was the same man who'd been his mentor so many years ago.

Hank stepped forward, holding out his hand. "Morgan, I'm glad you made it. You must've driven all night to get here."

Drake took the man's hand and was pulled into a

bone-crunching hug.

"Good to see you," Hank said.

"Same," Drake said. "It's been a few years."

Hank stepped back. "I believe you know everyone here."

Drake nodded, his lips spreading into a grin.

A man with dark blond hair, blue eyes and a naturally somber expression stepped past Hank and pulled Drake into another powerful hug. "Dude, it's been too long."

"Grimm," Drake clapped his hand on the man's back. "I thought you were still on active duty."

Mike Reaper, or Grimm as he'd been aptly nicknamed, patted his leg. "Took shrapnel to my left leg. It bought me early retirement."

Drake shook his head. "Sorry to hear that."

"I'm not. I was getting too old to play with the young kids. It was time for me to move on." He nodded. "I'm looking forward to getting my hands dirty with something besides gun cleaning oil."

"Move over, Grimm. My turn." A man shoved Grimm to the side. "Bring it in, Morgan."

A black-haired man with shocking blue eyes grabbed Drake by the shoulders and crushed him in a hug. "'Bout time we worked together again," he said. "When did we last?"

"Afghanistan," Drake said when he could breathe again. He grinned at his old teammate from his last tour of duty before leaving the Navy. "We took out that Taliban terrorist who was cutting off heads for fun. How're you doing, Murdock?"

Sean Murdock stood back, smiling. "Better, now that you're here. Thought we were going to be Army puke heavy. We needed some bone frogs to level the playing field." He turned and dragged another man forward. "Remember this guy?"

Drake's brow furrowed. "Utah?"

The handsome man with the auburn hair and blue eyes smirked. "I prefer to go by Pierce. I like to think I've outgrown the Utah moniker."

Murdock laughed and pounded Utah on the back. "You'll never live down Utah. Once an uptight asshole, always an uptight asshole."

Pierce "Utah" Turner's lips pressed together. "Thanks." He held out his hand to Drake. "Good to see you under better circumstances than the last time we worked together."

Drake gripped the man's hand, truly glad to see him. "Taking mortar fire while trying to extract that Marine platoon was not one of our cleanest joint operations. You saved my life that day."

"And you returned the favor five minutes later," Utah said. "I'd call it even."

Drake glanced toward the last man he knew in the group and smiled. "Hey, Judge. You're a sight for sore eyes."

"Didn't think you'd remember me, it's been so long." Joe "Judge" Smith, former Delta Force Operative, was the old man of the group of men Drake would work with at the lodge. Like Hank, he'd influenced Drake when he was a young Navy SEAL fresh out of training. He'd been an integral part of the first joint operation of which Drake had been a part.

He'd hung back to provide cover fire for the team as they'd exited a hot zone. Judge had taken a bullet to his right forearm and had to use his left arm and hand to fire his rifle. The man hadn't missed a beat. He'd held on long enough for the entire team to reach the Black Hawk helicopters waiting at the extraction point.

When Judge hadn't been right behind them loading the aircraft, Drake had jumped out, determined to go back. He'd gone less than twenty yards when Judge had come running, dozens of Taliban soldiers on his heels.

Drake and the rest of his team had provided him cover until he'd dove aboard the helicopter. They'd lifted off under heavy fire and made it back to the Forward Operating Base without losing a single man. He'd made an impression on Drake he would never forget.

"What brings you to Montana?" Drake asked.

"Got tired of wiping the noses of baby Deltas," Judge said. "When I reached my twenty, I figured it was time to leave."

"I always wondered why they called you Judge," Drake admitted.

Judge shrugged.

Grimm laughed. "It came out of a barroom fight. Patterson didn't like the way a man was treating one of the ladies. When he told him to back off, the man asked him what he was going to do if he didn't." Grimm's lips curled. "He became the Judge, jury and executioner."

"You killed the guy?" the woman at the drafting table asked.

Judge shook his head. "No."

"He made him wish he was dead," Grimm said. "He almost got kicked out of Delta Force. If the woman he'd defended hadn't come forward to tell her side of the story, his career would've been over."

Drake glanced around at the men he'd fought with and shook his head. "Had I known we were having a reunion, I would've come sooner."

"I want each of you to know I would hire you in a heartbeat for my organization, Brotherhood Protectors, but you all have expressed your desire to fire nail guns, not Glocks. I haven't given up hope that you'll change your mind, but I respect that you want to try something different. And with that, I'll hand you over to your new bosses. Molly McKinnon and her fiancé, Parker Bailey, are from the Iron Horse Ranch." Hank waved a hand toward the man and the woman who'd remained at the drafting table. "They're the new owners of the Lucky Lady Lodge."

"For better or worse." The man took Drake's

hand. "Welcome aboard. I'm here to do the grunt work, just like you guys." He turned to the woman. "Molly is the brains behind the project."

Molly shook Drake's hand. "Glad to meet you. Now, if we could get started…"

He smiled. "Yes, ma'am."

She turned to the drawings. "We're in the demolition phase of this project. We have to clean up what was damaged in the mine explosion before we can assess structural damage," Molly said.

Parker added. "Each man has been assigned different areas to work, not too far from each other in case you run into trouble."

Molly pointed to the blueprint. "Drake, you'll take the butler's pantry and coat closet on the far side of the main dining room. The walls are cracked and crumbling. We need to get behind the drywall to see if the support beams have been compromised. Your goal today is to clear the walls on the mountainside of the rooms and any other walls showing significant damage."

Parker raised a hand. "I'll take Drake and Grimm to their locations."

Molly glanced toward the other three men. "The rest are with me. You'll find sledgehammers, battery-powered reciprocating saws, gloves and wheelbarrows staged in each of your areas. The power is off, so you'll have to use the headlamps on your safety helmets. The rooms against the mountain don't get

236

much natural light." She handed Drake a helmet with a headlamp. "Thank you all for answering Hank's call. We needed as many hands as we could get for this project, and sometimes, people are hard to come by in small towns."

Anxious to get to work, Drake plunked his helmet on his head and followed Parker through the maze of hallways to the back of the lodge. They hadn't gone far before they had to stop and turn on their headlamps.

Parker continued, explaining what each room was as they passed doorways. He eventually came to a stop in front of a wooden door. "Grimm, this is your assigned area. Judge, yours is the next room. I'll be two doors down. If something doesn't feel right, get the hell out. We don't know exactly how much damage the explosion caused. I'd rather we err on the side of caution. The sooner we see inside the walls, the sooner we can get to work rebuilding."

"Got it." Grimm pulled on a pair of gloves, wrapped his hands around the handle of a sledge-hammer and nodded. "Nothing like a little demolition to work out all your frustrations. Let's do this."

Judge entered the next room and found what he needed to get started. Parker moved on.

Gloves on, Drake grabbed the sledgehammer and went to work knocking big holes in the plaster on the back wall. Piece by piece, he pulled away the plaster and the narrow wooden slats behind it, exposing a couple of feet of the interior beams at a time.

Plaster dust filled the air, making it more and more difficult to see. Judge found face masks in the stack of supplies and pulled one on over his mouth and nose. He'd made it through half the back wall in less than an hour. If he kept up the pace, he'd have that wall done in the next hour. The other walls in the room had only hairline fractures in the plaster. Hopefully, that was a good sign that they hadn't been damaged to the point they needed to be torn down as well.

One thing was certain; they'd have to wait until the dust settled before they could assess the status of the support beams.

The banging on the wall in the next rooms stopped for a moment.

"Can you see anything?" Grimm called out.

"Not much," Drake responded. "My headlamp is reflecting off all the dust particles."

"Same," Grimm came to stand in the doorway, wearing a mask over his mouth and nose.

"Let the dust settle for a few minutes," Parker called out.

"Have you had a chance to find a place to live?" Grimm asked.

Drake shook his head, his light swinging right then left, bouncing off the dust in the air. "I just got to town and came straight here."

"I think there's room at Mrs. Dottie Kinner's bed and breakfast where I'm staying. You can follow me there after work and ask her yourself if she's got another room available."

"Thanks." Drake glanced across the room. "I think I can see the wall again."

Grimm nodded. "Going back to my wall."

Moments later, the men were slamming their heavy sledgehammers into yet more plaster.

Drake worked on the next four feet of wall, knocking out sheetrock. He grabbed hold of a portion of the drywall and pulled hard. A large portion fell away, exposing a gap between studs that was three feet wide.

Had there been a door there at one time? He removed the rest of the plaster down to the floor and had to wait for the dust to settle in order to see the beams, much less if anything lay beyond the beams.

As the dust slowly settled, Drake's headlamp beam cut through the remaining particles to a room beyond the wall. It wasn't more than six feet by six feet square and had been carved out of the rock wall of the mountain.

He stepped between the beams into the stone-walled room. Several wooden crates littered the floor, along with a pile of what appeared to be clothing. He crossed to the crates and found them to be full of bottles of some kind of liquid. None of the bottles were labeled.

Drake suspected the bottles were moonshine and that the stash was left over from the Prohibition Era. He turned the beam of his headlamp to the pile of clothes on the floor. The cloth had a floral pattern of faded pink and yellow. Perhaps it had once been a curtain or a woman's dress.

As he neared the pile, he noticed a shoe and something that appeared to be a pole or thick stick lying beside it.

His pulse picked up, his empty belly roiling. He leaned over the pile of clothes and the shoe and froze.

The stick wasn't a stick at all. It was a bone. On the other side of it was another bone just like it.

With the handle of his sledgehammer, he moved the crate beside the pile of cloth and gasped.

On the other side of the crate, lying against the cold stone floor, lay a skull covered in a dry mummified layer of skin with a few long, thin strands of hair clinging to it in scattered patches.

"Parker," Drake called out.

When the hammering continued, Drake cleared his throat and yelled. "Parker!"

All hammering ceased.

"That you, Drake?" Parker answered.

With his gaze on what he now had determined was a complete skeleton covered in a woman's dress, Drake said, "You need to come see this."

ABOUT THE AUTHOR

ELLE JAMES also writing as MYLA JACKSON is a *New York Times* and *USA Today* Bestselling author of books including cowboys, intrigues and paranormal adventures that keep her readers on the edges of their seats. When she's not at her computer, she's traveling, snow skiing, boating, or riding her ATV, dreaming up new stories. Learn more about Elle James at www.ellejames.com

Website | Facebook | Twitter | GoodReads | Newsletter | BookBub | Amazon

Or visit her alter ego Myla Jackson at mylajackson.com
Website | Facebook | Twitter | Newsletter

Follow Me!
www.ellejames.com
ellejamesauthor@gmail.com

ALSO BY ELLE JAMES

Shadow Assassin

Delta Force Strong

Ivy's Delta (Delta Force 3 Crossover)

Breaking Silence (#1)

Breaking Rules (#2)

Breaking Away (#3)

Breaking Free (#4)

Breaking Hearts (#5)

Breaking Ties (#6)

Breaking Point (#7)

Breaking Dawn (#8)

Breaking Promises (#9)

Brotherhood Protectors Yellowstone

Saving Kyla (#1)

Saving Chelsea (#2)

Saving Amanda (#3)

Saving Liliana (#4)

Saving Breely (#5)

Saving Savvie (#6)

Saving Jenna (#7)

Brotherhood Protectors Colorado

SEAL Salvation (#1)

Rocky Mountain Rescue (#2)

Ranger Redemption (#3)

Tactical Takeover (#4)

Colorado Conspiracy (#5)

Rocky Mountain Madness (#6)

Free Fall (#7)

Colorado Cold Case (#8)

Fool's Folly (#9)

Colorado Free Rein (#10)

Rocky Mountain Venom (#11)

Brotherhood Protectors

Montana SEAL (#1)

Bride Protector SEAL (#2)

Montana D-Force (#3)

Cowboy D-Force (#4)

Montana Ranger (#5)

Montana Dog Soldier (#6)

Montana SEAL Daddy (#7)

Montana Ranger's Wedding Vow (#8)

Montana SEAL Undercover Daddy (#9)

Cape Cod SEAL Rescue (#10)

Montana SEAL Friendly Fire (#11)

Montana SEAL's Mail-Order Bride (#12)

SEAL Justice (#13)

Ranger Creed (#14)

Delta Force Rescue (#15)

Dog Days of Christmas (#16)

Montana Rescue (#17)

Montana Ranger Returns (#18)

Hot SEAL Salty Dog (SEALs in Paradise)

Hot SEAL, Hawaiian Nights (SEALs in Paradise)

Hot SEAL Bachelor Party (SEALs in Paradise)

Hot SEAL, Independence Day (SEALs in Paradise)

Brotherhood Protectors Boxed Set 1

Brotherhood Protectors Boxed Set 2

Brotherhood Protectors Boxed Set 3

Brotherhood Protectors Boxed Set 4

Brotherhood Protectors Boxed Set 5

Brotherhood Protectors Boxed Set 6

Iron Horse Legacy

Soldier's Duty (#1)

Ranger's Baby (#2)

Marine's Promise (#3)

SEAL's Vow (#4)

Warrior's Resolve (#5)

Drake (#6)

Grimm (#7)

Murdock (#8)

Utah (#9)

Judge (#10)

The Outriders

Homicide at Whiskey Gulch (#1)

Hideout at Whiskey Gulch (#2)

Held Hostage at Whiskey Gulch (#3)

Setup at Whiskey Gulch (#4)

Missing Witness at Whiskey Gulch (#5)

Cowboy Justice at Whiskey Gulch (#6)

Hellfire Series

Hellfire, Texas (#1)

Justice Burning (#2)

Smoldering Desire (#3)

Hellfire in High Heels (#4)

Playing With Fire (#5)

Up in Flames (#6)

Total Meltdown (#7)

Declan's Defenders

Marine Force Recon (#1)

Show of Force (#2)

Full Force (#3)

Driving Force (#4)

Tactical Force (#5)

Disruptive Force (#6)

Mission: Six

One Intrepid SEAL

Two Dauntless Hearts

Three Courageous Words

Four Relentless Days

Five Ways to Surrender

Six Minutes to Midnight

Hearts & Heroes Series

Wyatt's War (#1)

Mack's Witness (#2)

Ronin's Return (#3)

Sam's Surrender (#4)

Take No Prisoners Series

SEAL's Honor (#1)

SEAL'S Desire (#2)

SEAL's Embrace (#3)

SEAL's Obsession (#4)

SEAL's Proposal (#5)

SEAL's Seduction (#6)

SEAL'S Defiance (#7)

SEAL's Deception (#8)

SEAL's Deliverance (#9)

SEAL's Ultimate Challenge (#10)

Texas Billionaire Club

Tarzan & Janine (#1)

Something To Talk About (#2)

Who's Your Daddy (#3)

Love & War (#4)

Billionaire Online Dating Service

The Billionaire Husband Test (#1)

The Billionaire Cinderella Test (#2)

The Billionaire Bride Test (#3)

The Billionaire Daddy Test (#4)

The Billionaire Matchmaker Test (#5)

The Billionaire Glitch Date (#6)

The Billionaire Perfect Date (#7) coming soon

The Billionaire Replacement Date (#8) coming soon

The Billionaire Wedding Date (#9) coming soon

Ballistic Cowboy

Hot Combat (#1)

Hot Target (#2)

Hot Zone (#3)

Hot Velocity (#4)

Cajun Magic Mystery Series

Voodoo on the Bayou (#1)

Voodoo for Two (#2)

Deja Voodoo (#3)

Cajun Magic Mysteries Books 1-3

SEAL Of My Own

Navy SEAL Survival

Navy SEAL Captive

Navy SEAL To Die For

Navy SEAL Six Pack

Devil's Shroud Series

Deadly Reckoning (#1)

Deadly Engagement (#2)

Deadly Liaisons (#3)

Deadly Allure (#4)

Deadly Obsession (#5)

Deadly Fall (#6)

Covert Cowboys Inc Series

Triggered (#1)

Taking Aim (#2)

Bodyguard Under Fire (#3)

Cowboy Resurrected (#4)

Navy SEAL Justice (#5)

Navy SEAL Newlywed (#6)

High Country Hideout (#7)

Clandestine Christmas (#8)

Thunder Horse Series

Hostage to Thunder Horse (#1)

Thunder Horse Heritage (#2)

Thunder Horse Redemption (#3)

Christmas at Thunder Horse Ranch (#4)

Demon Series

Hot Demon Nights (#1)

Demon's Embrace (#2)

Tempting the Demon (#3)

Lords of the Underworld

Witch's Initiation (#1)

Witch's Seduction (#2)

The Witch's Desire (#3)

Possessing the Witch (#4)

Stealth Operations Specialists (SOS)

Nick of Time

Alaskan Fantasy

Boys Behaving Badly Anthologies

Rogues (#1)

Blue Collar (#2)

Pirates (#3)

Stranded (#4)

First Responder (#5)

Blown Away

Warrior's Conquest

Enslaved by the Viking Short Story

Conquests

Smokin' Hot Firemen

Protecting the Colton Bride

Protecting the Colton Bride & Colton's Cowboy Code

Heir to Murder

Secret Service Rescue

High Octane Heroes

Haunted

Engaged with the Boss

Cowboy Brigade

Time Raiders: The Whisper

Bundle of Trouble

Killer Body

Operation XOXO

An Unexpected Clue

Baby Bling

Under Suspicion, With Child

Texas-Size Secrets

Cowboy Sanctuary

Lakota Baby

Dakota Meltdown

Beneath the Texas Moon